Weekly Reader Children's Book Club presents

The Three Toymakers

ALSO BY URSULA MORAY WILLIAMS

The Adventures of the Little Wooden Horse
Beware of This Animal
Boy in a Barn
A Crown for a Queen
The Cruise of the *Happy-Go-Gay*
The Earl's Falconer
Island MacKenzie
Johnnie Tigerskin
The Moonball
The Toymaker's Daughter

The Three Toymakers

by

URSULA MORAY WILLIAMS

Illustrated by Shirley Hughes

THOMAS NELSON INC.
New York   Camden

No character in this story is intended to represent any actual person; all the incidents of the story are entirely fictional in nature.

Library of Congress Catalog Card Number: 79-152875
ISBN 0-8407-6114-7 (trade); ISBN 0-8407-6115-5 (library)

Weekly Reader Children's Book Club Edition
Intermediate Division

Contents

The Three Toymakers

1

Peter Toymaker
and Young Rudi

One afternoon in early winter, old Peter Toymaker noticed a sharp pair of eyes gazing at him from over the top of his workbench.

The old toymaker was used to the stares of the village children, who often stopped in the street to peep inside his workshop and watch him at his work. For a long while he whittled away without paying much attention to the watcher, as he waited for the chatter and stream of questions that were bound to follow.

But the questions never came, and when he looked up he realized that the child who stood here was one he had never before seen. This was odd, because old Peter made toys for every child in the village.

He drove in five more nails and chipped away five more splinters before he spoke, and then it was only to say,

"Good afternoon, my little man."

"Good afternoon, Peter Toymaker," said the child cheerfully and politely.

Old Peter Toymaker could see no more than the eyes and nose of the boy who was staring at him. When he peered farther across the bench he noticed a patched coat, a pair of darned trousers, and an over-large pair of boots. And in spite of the patches and the darns there were holes in the boy's thin clothes.

It must be very cold to go about with so many windows open in wintry weather, thought old Peter Toymaker.

Darkness was falling. He took the coffeepot off the stove and called the child to come inside and warm himself.

"What is your name, my little man?" he asked, cutting two large slices of bread from the loaf.

"My name is Rudi," said the boy, accepting a slice of bread and a bowl of coffee with dignity. Wrapping his hands around the bowl he drank the hot coffee very quickly, but the bread remained uneaten on the bench.

"Aren't you hungry?" the old toymaker asked.

The boys eyes were traveling around the workshop.

"If I sweep the floor for you, will you give me another slice?" he asked.

Old Peter Toymaker was amused.

"Certainly I will, if you sweep it properly."

The boy seized the broom and flew about the room. Chips, shavings, sawdust were chased from the corners and swept into a tidy pile. Old Peter cut a second slice of bread, but the boy, accepting it politely, merely laid it on top of the first.

"What? Won't you eat that either?" said the toymaker, astonished.

"If I sort out your nails, will you give me a third slice?" the boy demanded.

Soon the nails were well sorted and a third slice lay beside the others. Still the boy looked eagerly around the room.

"Isn't there any more work to be done?" he asked.

"So it's work you are after, is it?" said old Peter Toymaker. "To tell the truth, I could do with a boy like you about the place. Would you like to come and work for me in my workshop?"

The boy's eyes sparkled.

"Yes indeed, I would!" he exclaimed.

"Well, then," said old Peter, "You can sleep in the attic and eat with me, and every Thursday you shall have a silver piece. A toymaker's trade is an excellent thing for a boy to learn, you know."

But the boy's face fell.

"I couldn't sleep in the attic," he said sadly.

"Are you afraid of the cold?" old Peter Toymaker asked. Then he looked at the boy's thin clothes and added kindly, "Well, you can have a bed behind the stove if you prefer it. It's all the same to me!"

But the boy looked ready to cry.

"I couldn't sleep behind the stove," he said with downcast eyes.

"Then be off with you!" said old Peter, losing patience. "I'll have no young princes in my workshop!" And he turned his back on the boy.

To his surprise Rudi stayed where he was, murmuring in a low voice,

"I would come very early in the morning. You wouldn't know I had ever been away."

"Oh," said the toymaker, looking at him again. "So you want to sleep at home, do you? Who is your father?"

"My father is dead," said Rudi.

"Well, then, your mother?"

"My mother is dead too."

"Surely you don't live alone?"

"No. I have a little brother . . ."

"So the two of you live together?"

"Well . . . I have two little brothers . . ."

"*Two* brothers?"

"Well sir, I have three little brothers . . ."

"All so young as that? Are there no more?"

"To tell you the truth, there is a fourth."

"My poor child, tell me the whole truth. Is that the rest of your family?"

"Well, the whole truth is that I have five little brothers all younger than myself."

"All fatherless and motherless!" said old Peter Toymaker, "I can hardly believe it . . ."

"And . . ."

"And what?" said Peter Toymaker. "Isn't that the end of the family after all?"

"No, sir. Besides my five little brothers I have a sister, but only one. She comes next to me in age. She is a cripple."

The kind old toymaker was stricken to the heart at the thought of such a large family all dependent on the earnings of one young boy. He discovered that they lived seven miles away, in a cottage on the side of the mountain.

"Why did you come to see me?" old Peter asked.

"Six years ago my father shot a bear," Rudi said. "He sold the pelt for several silver pieces. On his way home he came into your workshop and bought a doll for my sister. My father was one of the King's foresters, and when he died my mother received a small pension. But then she died too, and the pension is so small it is hardly enough to feed us. Last night my sister and I talked things over between us. We decided I should come to you and ask if you will apprentice me to become a toymaker. I would do all I could to be useful and help you, and meanwhile I would learn all you can teach me of the trade."

Old Peter was so pleased with young Rudi's courage and honesty that he promised there and then to give him a trial. Meanwhile he filled a basket with food and saw the boy off on his long walk through the forest to his mountain home.

To his surprise, when he came into his workshop in the morning young Rudi was already sweeping the floor, and all that day and every day after he worked like ten men from dawn till dusk. The old toymaker began to wonder how he had ever managed without him.

Every night he sent Rudi home with a basket of good things for his family.

"Aren't you frightened in the forest at night?" he asked him now and then.

"No, I'm not frightened," Rudi said.

"Not of the trolls and the goblins?"

"Why should they trouble me?"

"What about the bears and the wolves that prowl in the forest?"

"My sister prays for me all the time I am away," Rudi said simply. "So it is not possible for any harm to come to me."

"You are a good boy," said old Peter Toymaker. "But I will give you some advice. You must make friends with the trolls and the goblins, so that they will help you when you need them. And you must study the habits and the ways of the bears and the wolves until you are cleverer than they are. If you do this, your sister's prayers will always be answered and nothing will hurt you."

∾§ 2 §∾

The Toymakers

Six years had passed. Young Rudi was eighteen now, his shoulders broad, his legs long, and his cheeks ruddy. It was difficult to believe he had ever been so small that he could only peep over the top of old Peter Toymaker's workbench. He was the boldest hunter in the village and the bravest climber in the mountains.

And what a toymaker Rudi had become! Old Peter had taught him all he knew of the trade, and loved him like a son.

Rudi's wooden bears opened their mouths so realistically they actually seemed to roar, while his carved swallows almost flew. All the little girls in the village wanted to own one of Rudi's dolls, they were so life-like, and his puppets were the nicest the children had ever seen.

Rudi had taken the old toymaker's advice and made friends with the trolls and the goblins in the forest. They showed him where the best toy-carving timber grew, and in return he often made miniature baskets and cradles and benches which he left among the undergrowth to please them.

Little by little he took over the heavier work from old Peter, who now had leisure to sit in the sun talking to his neighbors and to the children, particularly the five brothers of his adopted son Rudi, who were growing into strong, healthy boys, nearly as useful and busy as their eldest brother.

A few years ago Rudi had brought his whole family down to live in the village, so that he could work for longer hours at the workbench and be close at hand to look after old Peter Toymaker, who was beginning to suffer from failing eyesight and twinges of rheumatism in his back and legs. The new house was much more convenient for Rudi's crippled sister, Elsa, who soon became the favorite of everyone in the village, for she was so cheerful, unselfish and uncomplaining. Always ready to help people, she never failed to smile and to wave to her neighbors as she sat at the window repairing her brothers' clothes or sewing shirts.

The boys were growing up now, and leaving home. The two eldest after Rudi had gone to become soldiers, the next was apprenticed to a blacksmith. The fourth was still at school. He was the brightest of the family and wanted to study law.

Anders, the youngest, could hardly be said to be still at school, for most of the time he was playing truant. He was both the despair and the delight of Rudi and Elsa, and the apple of old Peter's eye. The child worshiped the old toymaker almost as much as he did his brother Rudi. He was only waiting for the day when he could officially leave school and learn the toymaking trade. He had no doubt at all that he would become the most famous toymaker in the world.

Meanwhile he dogged the footsteps of old Peter and Rudi from morning till night. When he was sent off to school he often slipped into the forest to join his friends the trolls and the goblins, who loved him both for his own sake and because he was Rudi's brother.

Now that there was Rudi Toymaker as well as old Peter Toymaker, the toys from the village of Drüssl became famous for many miles around. Yet old Peter and Rudi were not the only toymakers in a

district that provided trees of such an excellent quality for toymaking.

In the next village, Pils, there lived another toymaker, called Malkin. He was a very different kind of person. To begin with, he had no ordinary workshop like old Peter and Rudi. He had a window with bottle glass in it, just like a big city toyshop. And his toys were very exciting, although mothers and fathers did not approve of them at all.

He sold tricks and surprises and practical jokes. He sold eggs that burst with a bang when handled, releasing a terrible smell, candles that went out in the dark, and small boxes which, when put under a stranger's pillow, groaned and wailed and caterwauled all night long. He sold hideous masks and false teeth and whiskers that transformed the most handsome face into an ugly monster. But his dolls were the worst. They scowled and leered and squinted, and yet the strange thing was that these hideous toys had a peculiar fascination for every child who saw them.

Small boys longed to spend their pocket money on the popguns that spurted ink, and the musical in-

struments that set every dog in the district howling. Little girls begged their mothers,

"Can't I have just *one* bad doll, Mother? All mine are so terribly good!"

The children of Drüssl were forbidden to go to Malkin's shop, but go they did, and many a home was disorganized by the tricks and jokes that the toymaker of Pils made and sold.

One of Malkin's chief admirers was young Anders, who could not stay away from his window. The two-mile walk to the next village meant nothing to him. Often when his elder brother and sister thought he was in school, Anders' nose was pressed against Malkin's shop window as he spent imaginary fortunes on the goods displayed.

He seldom had any pocket money to spend. Rudi had early learned to be thrifty and had taught his younger brothers that money was to be earned, not given away. Now and then he paid Anders a penny for sweeping out the workshop, but it was old Peter Toymaker who spoiled the boy and sometimes slipped some pennies into his hand. Then Anders felt rich indeed.

Though his conscience might prick him for spending his money at Malkin's shop, he quickly forgot to feel guilty, and was careful to keep his purchases out of sight. He did not want to upset anybody.

Even his schoolfellows could only guess who filled the inkpots with a strange ink that bubbled and boiled, and spurted from the inkpots in blots that spattered the copybooks without anybody dipping a pen into it. And when a pot of honey was passed around the school, and all their tongues stuck to the roofs of their mouths for a whole afternoon, Anders became as speechless as the rest of them, and just as surprised too at the strange effect the honey had upon them all. His last purchase had been a horn with a note so like a cow in pain that it sent all the neighbors rushing to their cowsheds when they heard it.

But in spite of his love of practical jokes, Anders was very popular. He was so willing and warm-hearted, always ready to run errands or do anybody a good turn. If he sometimes dawdled on the way or forgot what he had been sent for, nobody had the heart to blame him—he was always so sorry for his mistakes and he meant so well.

Anders was devoted to his lame sister, Elsa, but Rudi was his hero. He followed him whenever he could, and tried to copy everything he did.

About this time Rudi fell in love with the school-master's daughter Margaret, who was Elsa's best friend. People began to talk about wedding bells, and soon everybody in the village knew that Rudi Toy-maker and Margaret, the schoolmaster's daughter, would be married as soon as Rudi had earned enough money to set up house. This was not so simple a matter as it might seem, for although Rudi was no longer old Peter's apprentice but his partner, there were a great many demands on his purse.

He had to pay the burgomaster a certain sum every

year for the rent of his house. He had to save what he could spare for the school fees of Hans, the clever boy, who would certainly go to a university, after which Rudi would have to buy him a lawyer's practice.

Then the boy who was apprenticed to a blacksmith was growing at such a rate that he needed new clothes twice a year. He also wore out a quantity of shoe leather on his holidays, tramping to and from the distant village where he worked. And Rudi had to pay a substantial amount for the boy's food and lodging too.

Besides this, he and Elsa liked to send a piece of silver now and again to the two young soldier brothers, who were serving in the King's army.

Anders too must be clothed and fed and his school fees paid, although he constantly asked to be allowed to leave school and become a toymaker. This usually ended in his elder brother's boxing his ears and giving him a handful of chips to carve into birds and animals, which Anders did very fairly.

Their sister Elsa earned enough money by dressmaking to clothe herself and help to pay the rent, but cooking and mending for her brothers took much of her time, and often she was too tired to undertake all the work that might have come her way.

So there was not much hope of an early wedding for Rudi and his Margaret, but they were content to wait and passed the time as happily as any pair of lovers with much to look forward to and no regrets behind them. Elsa was delighted to think that her best friend was going to be her sister. She worked hard at her dressmaking, hoping to earn enough money to buy a roll of fine linen with which she intended to make embroidered sheets and pillowcases for Rudi and Margaret.

All the family was pleased about the coming marriage except Anders, who found that Rudi was now too occupied to pay much attention to him. Anders became so depressed that for several weeks he even went regularly to school and rose to be top of his class.

Then he decided to fall in love himself, choosing for his sweetheart little Janni from the mill, who was too young to go to school. This made a good excuse for missing a class or two.

"What? Did they let you out early again, Anders?" Janni's mother asked, doling out slices of gingerbread as he and Janni sat side by side on the steps of the mill. "Were you top of the class again? What a clever man you will become!"

Anders was ashamed to admit in front of Janni that he had sunk to the bottom of the class once more. He filled his mouth with gingerbread and said nothing at all. Janni's mother smiled at them kindly and went indoors.

3

The Toys

News came to the village of Drüssl in a proclamation pinned up on a tree near the burgomaster's house.

"The King is offering a thousand gold pieces as a prize!" shouted Anders when he had read it. "A thousand gold pieces for a single toy! All the toymakers in the world will compete for it and our Rudi will win!"

Anders might have spoken wildly in his enthusiasm, but at least all the toymakers in the kingdom were invited to compete for the King's prize. They might enter any toy they chose to make. As judges the King had appointed the young Princess, and the daughter of a woodcutter in his forest.

Nothing else was talked of for weeks in the village of Drüssl, where every man, woman, and child took a pride in the work of their master toymakers, old Peter and Rudi. At first old Peter smiled and said that his day for such things was past, but his family would not hear of such nonsense, and when he saw

Rudi trying and testing the best wood and sharpening his tools, the old man changed his mind and became just as interested in the project as his adopted son.

This gave Rudi great pleasure, and the two toy-makers spent their days side by side at the work-bench, absorbed in working out their own ideas, sharing their tools and the companionship that had grown even closer between them as the years went by.

Anders promptly told Janni that he too meant to enter the King's competition. Rudi good-humoredly gave him wood, nails, paint, and glue, and Anders had his own sharp knife and a little hammer. He played truant more often than ever, sitting on the millsteps under the admiring eyes of little Janni, carving toy after toy that never reached completion because he forever wanted to start something new. The mill steps were littered with chips, and legless wooden horses and headless birds floated mournfully down the millstream to be whirled away under the great wheel.

Janni's mother still gave him gingerbread, but she guessed it was not his position in class that gave him so many holidays.

"If Rudi wins the prize, he and Margaret will be married," Anders told Janni. "I shall wear a new blue coat at the wedding with silver buttons on it, and silver buckles on my shoes. But if I win, then you and I will be married at once and I will buy you a basket of sweetmeats and a golden spinning wheel. I will build you a little house in the forest and we will invite all the trolls and the goblins to our housewarming. Won't that be nice?"

But Janni said she did not want to leave her mother.

"Oh, well, then I will give you a basket of sweetmeats just the same," said Anders kindly.

The summer passed. Autumn came, and Elsa's brothers brought scarlet berries to her room. Red and yellow toadstools appeared in the forest. Little by little the roar of the great waterfall ceased as icicles screened the torrent, while the powerful millstream, swift as ever, was bordered by ice.

Elsa had made a new winter jacket for Anders from Rudi's old hunting coat. He went to show it off to Janni, but it was too cold now to sit outside on the steps of the mill. He ran back to the workshop, where he never tired of watching Rudi and old Peter carving their marvelous toys.

Old Peter was making a dolls' house, but not the ordinary kind of plaything. In his house the wide roof, the wooden balcony, and the green shutters were carved as beautifully as on any of the real houses in the village. Small painted flowers swung in baskets from the beams, while under the eaves hung swallows' nests the size of thimbles. Close beside them clustered the swallows themselves, their delicate, pointed tails trembling in a draft from the open door.

One could have stared forever at the outside of this beautiful house, but the inside was still more wonderful. At a touch the whole of the front swung back to expose two rooms, one above and one below. They were so homelike and true to life that every child in the village could imagine himself back in his own house just by looking at them.

The downstairs room was, of course, the cowshed, crossed by beams the thickness of your thumb. On the beams perched a number of wooden cocks and hens, some with their heads tucked underneath their painted wings, some peering down at the cows below. A handsome cock, all green and gold, stood flapping his wings with his beak wide open to crow for all the world as if it were five o'clock in the morning. The cows were just as lifelike, though the largest could stand in a man's cupped hand. Painted tan, brown, red, and black, they munched at their mangers as old Peter had carved them, waiting for morning.

Upstairs was the living room, warmed by a tiny stove in which glowed lumps of charcoal painted red. The poster beds, chairs, tables, cupboards, and chests were all so perfect they might have been the work of goblin carpenters. There were tiny brooms in the corner, an ax one inch long, a chopping block, a pile of chips for firewood. The smallest gun in the world hung over the door.

Anders spent half of his time admiring this marvel of architecture. When the house was shut up he peered through the windows. When it was open he gazed to his heart's content. When old Peter Toymaker pinned up a bear's pelt the size of an autumn leaf on the dolls'-house walls and added a loaf of bread no bigger than a penny to the table, Anders leaped around the workshop crying,

"Bravo, Uncle Peter! Good clever Uncle Peter! You will win! Just see if I don't tell the truth!"

But then he came to the bench where his brother was carving, and crept under his elbow to admire his work in turn. Rudi was making a musical box, but nothing so ordinary as the kind one buys in city shops.

This box was a marvel, and there seemed no end to the tunes it could play. Rudi had carved the box from one of the oldest pines on the mountain. Helped by his friends the trolls and the goblins, he had spent a whole day going from tree to tree, tapping the trunks and listening to the music they made, to the strumming of the wind in their boughs, to the vibrations that ran up and down the boles from their roots. When he found the tree he wanted he felled it so carefully, with ax and saw and rope, that the tree sank to the ground with none of its music lost. Then he walked up and down the length of it, tapping the bole and listening until he found the best section. From this section he carved his musical box.

On the lid of the box were twenty or so little carved and painted figures, representing people from the village of Drüssl, as well as trolls and goblins from the forest with a charcoal burner, a woodcutter, and a huntsman with his dog and gun.

The burgomaster was there in his Sunday clothes, the baker with rolls of bread, the schoolmaster and half a dozen children from the school, including Anders. Little Janni was there in her white Sunday pinafore, and dear old Peter Toymaker carrying a string of puppets. There were also two soldiers looking exactly like Anders' elder brothers. None of these figures was any higher than a clothes peg. There were fir trees, painted shiny green, with fir cones on them, red toadstools spotted with white, and two wolves with quite a friendly look about their faces. There was even a brown bear standing on his hind legs, and when Rudi wound up the musical box, all these little figures *danced!*

No wonder that the workshop was thronged with children from morning to night and that nobody could make up his mind which of the two wonderful toys was the better!

❧ 4 ❧

Marta

The whole village had been so absorbed in the work of their own master toymakers that they had not given much thought as to what might be going on elsewhere. It was Anders who brought the news from Pils that Malkin too was entering the contest for the King's prize. Dropping everything, the whole village clustered around him as he stood beside the pump, swelling with importance at being the center of so much attention.

"What is he making, Anders?" came a chorus of eager voices. "And how is he making it?"

At first Anders hemmed and hawed, greatly enjoying the sensation he was causing in Drüssl.

"Malkin implored me not to tell a soul," he said. "You see, I saw it quite by accident as I happened to be passing by. I really think I had better say no more about it."

At once a clamor arose from every man, woman, and child in the village square.

"I'll give you five of my currant buns, Anders, if you tell us what you saw!" said the baker.

"I'll find you a button for your cap," the tailor promised.

"My old cat has kittens! You can take your choice," said an old dame, and Janni's mother called out,

"Speak up, Anders, and I'll bake you a gingerbread man."

Anders put his fingers in the sides of his waistcoat and was just about to open his mouth when Rudi's voice came ringing across the heads of the crowd.

"If you promised not to tell, Anders, you had better hold your tongue!"

But Anders was not to be subdued, even by his elder brother.

"Why, I never promised at all," he said airily. "For Malkin knows all about your wonderful singing box and the house that Uncle Peter is making, so how could he expect to keep his own work a secret after that?"

"Tell us, Anders! Tell us!" urged the crowd, and even Rudi listened as Anders told.

Malkin was making a doll.

"Oh, is that all?" said the crowd, quite relieved, because nobody in his senses could compare one of Malkin's hideous babies with old Peter's house or Rudi's singing box.

But it was not one of his usual dolls, Anders insisted. This one was very beautiful! Her skin was white and her hair as black as a raven's wing. Her lips were redder than wild strawberries and carved in the loveliest smile.

"And doesn't she squint or put her tongue out, Anders?" asked the unbelieving people of Drüssl.

She did nothing of the kind, Anders assured them. Her black eyes had long silky lashes that swept her cheeks. Gold earrings hung from her ears and she was as beautiful as a queen, said Anders.

"Oh, well, anyone can make a doll," said the scornful villagers.

But she walked! Anders said that when Malkin wound up her heart with a tiny key, she got up and strutted around the toyshop.

The villagers opened their eyes at that, but after all, walking dolls had been heard of before.

But she talked! Anders had kept this piece of information to the end. He described how the doll began to speak in the most natural manner possible. Her voice was like a silver bell, he said.

"What does she say, Anders?" they asked him.

"She says everything, just like a lady," said Anders. "She says long poems and sings like a nightingale!"

Suddenly Anders began to laugh, as if it were the funniest thing in the world to meet a doll who could speak and recite and sing like a nightingale. He laughed and laughed with such infectious peals that soon he had the whole village laughing with him.

Even Rudi had a smile on his face when he went back to the workshop to tell old Peter what all the commotion was about, but he seemed a little puzzled, as if he could not quite understand what Anders had found so amusing to laugh about.

If he had known all that Anders had seen, he certainly would not have laughed. For Anders, peeping through a crack in the roof of Malkin's toyshop, had watched Malkin winding up the doll faster and faster, with a cunning smile on his face, and when he removed the key she began to talk at the top of her voice, but not at all like a lady! The words she began with were the phrases little boys fling at each other when their mothers are out of hearing: "Pig-face! Cow's foot! Go and teach your grandmother to suck eggs!" and so forth. She went on to the angry expressions neighbors use between themselves when they are quarreling, and last of all she said all the rude and wicked names she could think of, for five minutes, without stopping, quite shocking Anders, who had been nicely brought up.

He slid from the roof and ran home as fast as his legs would carry him. But now that he was safe among his friends, the whole adventure struck him as being wonderfully funny, and it was not long before he had whispered the story into the ear of Pauli, his best school friend, from where it traveled very

quickly into the ears of all the other boys in the village.

That evening there was not a boy left in the village of Drüssl. Cats slept peacefully on their doorsteps. The two toymakers worked without interruption at their benches. They had never known such peace before.

But in the neighboring village of Pils, Malkin's toyshop was besieged by a noisy crowd of children, who drummed with their fingers on the window, peeped through the keyhole, and flattened their noses on the panes. A few of the braver ones even climbed onto the roof with Anders, but Malkin had mended the hole and there was nothing to be seen that way.

The toymaker locked the door and pulled the curtains across the window, but still the children clamored and drummed and demanded to be let in.

At last he could stand it no longer.

"What do you want?" he shouted, coming to the door.

"We want to see the doll!" the boys shouted. "We want to see the doll that walks and talks!"

By now the children from Drüssl had been joined by all the little boys in Malkin's own village. It really looked as if between them they might break down

the door of the toyshop if Malkin did not give them what they wanted.

"What doll?" he grumbled. "I have fifty dolls in my shop!"

"No! No!" clamored the children. "We want to see the doll you are making for the King's prize! The doll that walks and talks and sings like a nightingale!"

"Pigface!" called out a voice from the back of the crowd. "Pigface! Cow's foot! Go and tell your grandmother to suck eggs!" Malkin cast one look of venom at Anders, for the voice was his, and then grudgingly opened the door and beckoned the children into the back of the shop, where he was working by candlelight.

The doll sat primly beside the workbench like any well-behaved little girl. As Malkin brought in the children, she rose and curtsied, strutting before them like a little princess. You would hardly believe she was not made of flesh and blood.

As Anders had said, she was very beautiful. Her white skin, red lips, and sparkling eyes were very different from the grimaces Malkin painted on the rest of his dolls.

"Good evening, children," she greeted them in her high, clear voice.

The children stared and stared.

"What else can she say?" they asked as she sat down again.

When Malkin saw the respect and admiration on their faces he became quite pleasant.

"I will wind her up a little more and you shall see for yourselves," he told them.

He took a small silver key from the chain that hung around his neck and fitted it into a keyhole under the doll's left arm.

Immediately she began to recite very prettily:

> "Little children, 'tis the rule
>   You should love your work at school.
>   Happiness rewards the worker,
>   Only misery the shirker."

"Does she always say the same verses?" the children asked.

"No, indeed!" said Malkin proudly. "Tell them another poem, my dear!"

"I will say a poem about the wind," the doll said primly.

She began:

> "I am young! I am old!
>   I am shy! I am bold!
>   I am wild! I am free!
>   The whole wide world is a home for me!
>   I can break! I can bend!
>   I can kill! I can rend!
>   And never a soul can capture me!"

The children liked this poem, but Malkin appeared a little vexed.

"You might have chosen something better than that, my dear," he said to the doll.

The boys all clapped their hands and begged for more.

"You may sing them a song," Malkin told the doll.

"You must wind me up again," she said crossly. "I am running down!"

"Well, just a little," said Malkin. "One has to be careful at first," he explained to the children. "The delicate springs are so stiff."

Now the doll leaped and sprang all over the shop in her delight at being wound up again. The children shouted with excitement at seeing her.

"Hush!" Malkin reproved them. "You will over-excite her. Sing to us, my dear."

The voice that rose to Malkin's roof was as beautiful as a nightingale's. The children listened, entranced, until she had finished.

"Sing again! Oh, do sing to us again!" they begged when the song was over.

Malkin was so flattered by their enthusiasm that he readily agreed to let the doll sing again.

"Sing the angel's song to the children," he told her.

But the doll pouted and grumbled.

"You must wind me up again," she said. "How can I sing when my spring is running down?"

Malkin took out his key with ill grace and wound her up again. "Why, you are not nearly run down yet," he exclaimed as he turned the key.

Now the doll leaped and bounded and capered, turning head over heels with the grace of a wild young panther. When at last she became quieter she burst into song—not the song of the angels, but a wild bandit's ditty that roused the children's spirits and set them roaring out the chorus. When she had finished they shouted and stamped their approval, but once again Malkin looked vexed.

"That was not the song I told you to sing," he scolded the doll angrily.

She put her face in her hands and burst into tears.

"Don't scold her, Malkin. Don't scold her," pleaded the boys. "Let her sing the angel's song to us now, to show she is sorry!"

"Oh, yes, I will! I will!" sobbed the doll. "Only I am quite, quite exhausted! Please wind me up a little, kind master, for I am almost run down!"

"Nonsense!" said the toymaker angrily. "I wound you up enough to sing at least twenty songs, and what you say is ridiculous!"

The doll only sobbed more bitterly.

"I have no strength left! I am quite, quite run down!" she repeated in a faint and helpless voice.

"Do wind her up! Oh, do wind her, Malkin!" the children begged, jumping and clapping their hands.

"Clever Malkin," added Anders, "Perhaps you will win the King's prize!"

At this the doll peeped at him between her fingers, giving him a wink that caused him to jump quite violently, but at the same time Malkin, with ill humor, took out his silver key and wound the doll up for the last time. After a few twists the key would turn no further.

"Why, you are fully wound up already!" cried the toymaker in a rage, but with a shout of joy the doll sprang out of his arms.

Chased by Malkin, she leaped from chair to bench and from bench to shelf, to the utter delight of the watching children. From the shelf she jumped onto the windowsill, finally perching on the beam that crossed the roof, where she closed her eyes, folded her hands, and began to sing the angel's song in a voice that was sweeter than a nightingale's.

But hardly were the children's spirits calmed, hardly had Malkin extricated himself from the tangle of benches and boxes where the chase had led him when the doll stopped suddenly in the middle of her song. Her hands unfolded, and her black eyes opened and began to flash.

"Pigface!" she screamed. "Cow's foot! Nutcracker! Your mother is a witch! Go and teach your grandmother to suck eggs!"

At first the children were startled by the sudden

change. Then they burst out laughing and at once the wicked doll broke into a stream of rude words that might have continued for some considerable time if Malkin had not made a great bound and caught her by the foot. The doll tumbled off the beam into the toymaker's hands, where she lay limp and silent, pretending to be broken.

"Miserable creature!" cried Malkin, shaking her till her legs and arms rattled. "How shall I punish you?"

"Why did you teach me such wicked things, master?" The doll sighed feebly, but once again she winked at Anders, whose warm heart held a lot of sympathy for her.

"I will make you perfect yet," the toymaker muttered, flinging her back on her stool. "I will make you into a lady and you shall win the King's prize for me."

"How can I be a lady when my clothes are so poor and shabby?" the doll complained. "If I had pretty clothes to wear I should only think and say pretty things. And the Princess is hardly likely to choose me in such a ragged dress as this. But there! I daresay you cannot afford anything better, master dear. One expects to pay a lot of money for the pretty things that Elsa the dressmaker—sister of young Anders here—makes for the people of Drüssl."

Malkin only scowled and bit his thumb.

Then he cleared all the little boys out of his shop and locked the door.

Anders ran back to bawl one last question through the keyhole.

"What is her name, Malkin? What is the doll's name?"

A shrill burst of laughter reached him from the back of the shop as the doll herself replied,

"My name is Marta," she told him.

5

Malkin Visits
the Dressmaker

Of course the news spread far and wide. Every day the little boys of Drüssl ran off to visit Malkin, and sometimes their elders went too, pretending that they were going to visit relatives.

Malkin would let nobody into the shop. The door was barred and bolted. Even those with money to spend were turned away. The curtains were drawn across the window, and the keyhole was blocked. Malkin even put wax on the roof so that it was too slippery to climb up on.

And then, after two weeks, a surprising thing happened. The door was unlocked, the curtains were drawn back, and there, in the middle of the shop window, sat the doll herself, as beautiful as ever, though she still wore her plain peasant's dress and old slippers. And as if that were not surprising enough, Malkin actually came to the door to welcome customers and invite them to come inside. He seemed only

too anxious, at last, to parade his doll and to show her off.

"Dance for the children, Marta," he told her, and she danced.

"Sing for them!" he commanded, and she sang.

Although Malkin wound her up as far as the key would turn, she never jumped about nor did anything that he did not order her to do. He had certainly turned her into a paragon of a doll. The children's parents admired her as they had never admired any of Malkin's work before.

"A pity," some of them remarked, "that the poor thing has no pretty dress to wear."

One afternoon lame Elsa sat in her chair looking out in the street, where the children were playing in the first fall of snow. She had finished her day's sewing and was about to light the lamp and make tea for her brothers when she noticed a dark figure, shrouded in a coat, dodging up the street from doorway to doorway as if it wished to avoid the rowdy boys throwing snowballs in the road.

To her great surprise the figure stopped at her door and rapped sharply on the knocker.

"Come in!" Elsa called, thinking this must be a friend come to find Rudi, who would soon be home.

The latch was lifted, and Malkin came in, stamping the snow off his boots. Elsa had never seen the toymaker from Pils before, but something about him repelled her. Gently and politely she asked his errand.

"Dear madam, I have heard of your fame as a dressmaker," Malkin began, warming his fingers at Elsa's fire. "People speak of you in the villages near and far!"

"That cannot be true," said Elsa seriously. "I have not enough time to do much work. I do make a few little dresses, it is true, for the children of Drüssl, but it is not likely that the news of them has spread far afield. What is it that you want?"

"Dear lady, I have a little daughter, seven years old," said the untruthful Malkin. "She has no mother, no one to make her the nice dresses little girls like to wear. I want her to have one frock, with gloves, socks, slippers, and underwear all complete. Could you undertake to make them, madam? They must be of the very best quality for my child, and I will pay well for them. Five gold pieces, madam, if you can have them ready in a week!"

Elsa's heart was touched at the thought of the motherless child. She never forgot the struggle she had had to clothe her little brothers.

"I would not need five gold pieces to dress a little child. Three would be enough," she said.

"Oh, but they must be of the finest materials," Malkin protested. "The slippers must be of satin and the stockings silk. There must be ribbons in all the petticoats, and the gloves must be made of real kid. As for the dress . . . well, dear madam, I am sure I can leave it to you to know what a little girl would like!"

"Why don't you go down to the city?" Elsa asked curiously. "You will find much better dressmakers there, and a choice of materials much finer than I have here at present."

"The dressmakers are all busy in the city," said Malkin, shaking his head. "They would never carry out my order in a week."

He knew well that most dressmakers would charge him five times as much as lame Elsa.

"Well, I will do my best," Elsa promised, thinking partly of the motherless child and partly of the linen for Rudi and Margaret's sheets that could be bought with the gold pieces.

"If you will bring your little girl to me, I will take her measurements," she added.

"I could not bring my delicate child through the forest in the snow!" said Malkin. "But I have all her measurements with me on this paper. I am sure you will find them all that you require!"

When Elsa examined the figures on the paper she was amazed at the small size of the hands and feet and the slimness of the doll's waist.

"What an exquisite little thing she must be," said Elsa. "It will be more like making clothes for a doll!"

"Why, yes, she is small and slight for her age," Malkin said nervously, preparing to leave. Elsa promised to do her best, and he departed as quickly as he had come.

The boys came home immediately after—Rudi, quiet and cheerful, Hans, loaded with books, and Anders, brimful of life, filling the room with laughter and snowflakes.

"What was Malkin doing here?" he asked, as he hung his jacket on a peg.

"*Malkin!*" Rudi and Hans exclaimed together. "Has that fellow been to the house?"

"I did not know it was Malkin!" Elsa exclaimed, nearly in tears. "He came to ask me to make some clothes for his little daughter."

"Malkin has no children," said Rudi. "What can he mean by that?"

But Anders burst out laughing.

"Why, it's for his doll Marta!" he cried. "The dress is for the doll he is making for the King's prize!"

"Then why did he deceive me so?" said Elsa indignantly, for she detested cheats and liars.

Anders said nothing. He guessed Malkin had been afraid that news of the doll's bad behavior had come to Drüssl, but none of the children had said anything about it. They were much too afraid of being forbidden to go and look at her again.

"Have nothing more to do with it," said Hans.

But Rudi said,

"If you have promised, you had better make the

clothes. Otherwise the people of Pils will say we are jealous, and trying to spoil their toymaker's chances. But do not charge him more than the cost of the materials, sister."

"Indeed, I will not," Elsa promised.

But she took no pleasure in making the exquisite little garments for her brother's rival. She had felt there was something unpleasant about Malkin from the first. She was so determined not to see him again that she had the clothes finished a day before he had asked for them, and sent Anders to Pils with them right after school.

They were as fine and dainty as anyone could ask for, each garment fit for a queen to wear. Anders said that Malkin was very pleased with them. He was also pleased at having to pay only three of the gold pieces he had offered.

Anders reported that the doll looked more beautiful than ever in her new finery. "Perhaps you have dressed the winner of the King's prize!" he added impishly.

"Oh, Anders, how can you say such a thing?" cried Elsa in anguish, but Anders put his arms around her neck.

"Well—haven't you dressed all the figures on Rudi's singing box?" he teased her, and Elsa was comforted.

But now that Malkin's doll not only behaved like a lady but looked like one, everyone had to admit that Malkin was a very serious rival to Rudi and old Peter Toymaker.

Malkin was so proud of her! He led her around the village of Pils on sunny days, parading her in front of the villagers, making her curtsy and greet everyone they met, her satin slippers covered with clogs and a cloak thrown over the pretty clothes Elsa had made for her.

The children from both villages adored her. Old Peter's workshop was often empty these days, but Malkin's toyshop never. Even the grown-ups grew quite fond of Malkin's doll. Her manners were so pretty they pointed her out as an example to their own children. Even the little boys began to forget that Marta had ever behaved badly.

So the days went on, until there were only ten remaining before the competition for the King's prize.

❧ 6 ❧

At the Palace

While the two villages, and many another village in the kingdom, were in a fever of excitement over the work of their craftsmen, tension was mounting high in the palace itself. The little Princess counted the day till the competition when she would see so many wonderful toys all set out together, for her to judge which was the best.

The King had wisely decided that this responsibility was to be shared by a child who was not so rich and fortunate as she, without the wealth of toys that filled the royal nursery. The time had come for the two young judges to meet each other and become acquainted. He invited the woodcutter's daughter, Anna, to spend an afternoon at the palace with the Princess. The following week the Princess would return the visit and spend some hours in the woodcutter's cottage.

The woodcutter's daughter was pale with shyness when her father brought her to the palace, but once the two children were left together they soon made friends and began eagerly to discuss the coming competition and all the wonderful toys they expected to see there.

"The dollmaker from Santa Felix is sure to bring some of his beautiful babies," the Princess told Anna. "Their eyes open and shut! Their legs and arms are so soft and round you would think they were real children. I know, because my father gave me one for a birthday present. But, oh dear! I dropped her in the lake and all her hair came out!"

"My father told me he heard that the toymaker from Lenzl is making a troupe of comical bears," said the woodcutter's daughter. "Each one is performing a different antic, he says, and they are all wonderfully carved and lifelike!"

"And I have heard of a swing from the village of Rippli all covered with little bells that play as you ride," continued the Princess. "Just think of all the space we shall need to show so many toys! My father is having the banquet hall arranged for the competition, and I am sure we shall need every inch of it. Have you ever heard of the marblemaker from Zwicklein? Every one of his glass marbles has a picture inside, though even the biggest is no larger than a walnut! And when you roll them across the table, snow falls on his trees and all his houses are as white as in winter. You ought to see his tiny reindeer galloping through the drifts!"

Anna, the woodcutter's daughter, had never heard of such wonderful toys as the Princess described. Neither had she seen such a vast collection as lined the royal nursery shelves.

The next week the Princess went to visit Anna at her cottage in the forest. Wearing a scarlet velvet hood to keep out the cold, she came riding in a sled lined with sealskin. But once inside the kitchen, she shed her little fur cloak and jumped about, quite delighted with all she saw.

She admired the quaint puppet Anna's father had

bought for her at a summer fair, and the carved goats and cows made by Anna's brother while he was guarding the flocks on the mountainside. She loved his pipes and whistles, decorated with sprays of fir or flowers, and the tiny wooden shoes, only fit for dolls, that hung along the chimney piece.

The children spent a happy afternoon together and parted the best of friends, eagerly looking forward to their next meeting, which would be on the day of the King's contest.

Anders and Marta

And now for the first time Rudi began to consider what it would mean to him to win the King's prize.

The honor, above all, would set him high above all the toymakers in the kingdom. His name would be famous forevermore. Then he and his Margaret could be married at once, and a new cottage built, big enough to hold all the family and old Peter Toymaker too, as the years slowly stole his strength away. Hans's future would be ensured, and Rudi could buy commissions for his young brothers in the army and help the apprentice to become a master blacksmith.

As for Anders, Rudi smiled tolerantly. He had an idea that the young rascal would need even more money than the others to set him up in life. A new chair would help Elsa, and she could have a spinning wheel at last, her heart's desire. In fact, the more he thought about all that the prize would bring to the

family, the more he longed, in spite of himself, to win
it.

In spite of himself, because Rudi knew that this
was old Peter Toymaker's last chance to make his
masterpiece. If he could win, he would die the hap-
piest man in the world, and Rudi's generous heart
could not grudge him such a reward. It was only
when caught off his guard that he told himself how
much more he needed both the honor and the
money.

Rudi had seen Malkin's doll, dressed in Elsa's
embroideries, stepping daintily down the street at
Malkin's side. Rudi nodded curtly, but Malkin
knew he had deceived Elsa and turned away his
head. If the doll was really as perfect as she looked,
then Rudi had to admit that Malkin was a serious
rival indeed.

The villagers thought so too. Some of their remarks
were almost ill-natured.

"Malkin has stolen a march on you this time,
Rudi."

"Who said Malkin could never make a perfect
toy? Some of us will have to sing a new tune."

Old Peter Toymaker refused to leave his workbench for the sake of looking at Malkin's masterpiece.
He did not pay much attention to Rudi's description.

"My boy," he said to Rudi, whom he still treated
as someone young and innocent at his knee, "I have

known Malkin for sixty years and you have only known him for eight. Believe me, he has *never* made a perfect toy!"

Anders became very concerned. He did not really care which one of his own nearest and dearest actually won the King's prize, but it was family pride that caused him such anxiety. Admittedly, old Peter's house was very beautiful and Rudi's singing box quite unique and extraordinary, but where had one ever seen a doll to rival Marta, now that she was so well dressed and had become as good as gold?

Malkin did not deserve to win.

Anders knew more about him than anyone else: he knew how Malkin rejoiced when his unpleasant tricks made people miserable; how he would go out of his way to speak spitefully of his neighbors behind their backs, or to do them a bad turn. So when Anders heard everyone praising the toymaker of Pils, and saying he had made a better toy than Rudi or old Peter, Anders boiled with indignation and began to think how he could defend his own dear ones and bring the wicked toymaker low.

Suddenly he took to going alone to Pils in the evenings, when the other boys had left the shop. He made himself useful to Malkin in small ways, and was always so polite and respectful that the toymaker became quite fond of him.

Marta too enjoyed his company, for he treated her as a person, instead of staring and pointing at her as the other boys did. She clapped her hands when she saw him coming down the street on his little skis, and gratefully accepted the nuts and sweets he brought her, for—oh yes! Malkin's doll could crunch a lollipop or crack a hazelnut in her white teeth like any schoolchild, and enjoyed it mightily too.

Malkin came to trust Anders, so that now and again he allowed him to take Marta for a walk down the street all alone, watching them carefully from the window all the while. Anders walked with a swagger, the envy of every child in the neighborhood, and the doll tripped gaily at his side. By now she was very fond of Anders.

But all this while, Anders was thinking of a plan. It was not one that Rudi would have approved of, but it must be remembered that Anders was very young and had been under Malkin's influence a great deal more than was good for him.

One Saturday morning Malkin locked up his shop with the doll inside it and set out alone to go to the nearest town. He was still perfecting the doll, and some silver wire was essential for his latest experiment. Anders offered to look after the shop in his absence, but Malkin smilingly refused.

"There is Marta," he said. "If someone came to steal her, you could hardly hold the shop alone against a gang of thieves!"

Malkin went off with the key of the toyshop in his pocket, while Anders peeped through the keyhole and saw Marta sitting on a chair, looking unhappy. She jumped up joyfully at his whistle.

"Come in, Anders! Come in!" she cried excitedly.

"Malkin has gone away and locked the door," Anders said. "Go and unbar the back window so I can climb inside!"

The doll willingly did as he asked. In a minute Anders had kicked the snow off his boots and was in the house.

Marta was delighted to see him, and for a while they amused themselves at playing cat's cradle and

sharing the little sugar biscuits that Malkin had left
for the doll while he was away. After a while, Anders
suggested that they should go for a little walk together in the street, but the doll refused. She said
Malkin had forbidden her to go outside without his
permission.

"You never used to trouble about what Malkin
said," observed Anders carelessly.

"Oh, I was very badly brought up in those days,"
the doll confessed. "Master has arranged the wires
and springs inside me so that now I never want to be
naughty. Besides, how could I be anything but good
and beautiful when I have such lovely clothes to
wear?"

"Your clothes are nice," Anders agreed, frowning
as he remembered how Malkin had tricked his sister. "But you still don't look quite like a lady. It is a
pity you have no smart necklace to wear."

"I have earrings," the doll said indignantly.

"Yes—oh yes! And your ears are very pretty.
Still, to my mind, you really ought to have a necklace
as well."

"Wretched boy," said the doll, nearly crying.
"Why did you put it into my head? I know my master will never give me one, for he keeps grumbling
about the amount he has spent on my clothes already."

"Oh, if that's all," said Anders carelessly, "I know
where you could get a necklace for nothing. There
are still some scarlet berries up the hill, just beyond

the village. I shook the snow from them this morning. They would make a very pretty necklace strung on a string for you to wear with your beautiful dress."

"Oh, do go and fetch them for me, dear, kind Anders," pleaded the doll, but Anders shook his head.

"They grow too high for me," he said. "It was when I was trying to reach them that I shook the snow off the bough. But if I were to lift you up, you could get them for yourself."

The doll danced in her excitement.

"Do you really think so, Anders? Let's go this minute! Just wait till I fetch my cloak. We can be back again before my master returns. How pleased he will be to see me in a beautiful necklace that has cost him nothing!"

The doll put on her cloak and clogs. The next moment the pair of them had climbed out of the window and were hurrying along the backs of the houses, not that anyone would have been surprised to see them out together. People were used to meeting them strolling hand in hand about the village streets.

When they left the village behind and began to climb the steep slopes beyond the houses, the doll complained,

"You did not tell me it was so far as this! Why do you walk so fast, Anders?"

"It isn't much farther," he told her briefly. "Think

of your beautiful necklace! You want to win the King's prize, don't you?"

"Indeed I do," said the doll with a smirk. "All the other dolls will look silly, won't they, when my master walks off with the bag of golden coins in his hand. How I shall laugh when they all go away disappointed!"

"It seems to me Malkin hasn't quite finished you yet," Anders said, looking at her sharply. "Now hurry up—we are nearly there."

"You hold my hand too tightly, Anders. You are hurting me," the doll complained. "You will have to carry me if you don't want me to fall down in the snow!"

Without a word, Anders picked her up in his arms and carried her until the slope eased off and they came to a small snowy plateau between fir trees.

"Where are the scarlet berries?" the doll asked, but for answer Anders whistled shrilly several times.

Suddenly there came a pattering sound and a rustling as fir branches were pushed aside and small brown hands appeared between the twigs. Curious brown faces peeped around the trunks. A sound of hurrying filled the steep forest as the goblins and trolls answered Anders' call and came swarming about him where he stood in the glade holding Marta by the hand.

The doll opened her black eyes in astonishment as she heard Anders say,

"My little friends and neighbors, I have brought you a queen! You can see how beautiful she is and she sings like a nightingale. Treat her well. Give her presents. Offer her your best treasures and your choicest food. Make her a necklace from the diamonds you dig out of the snow. Never let her leave you. Show her what a splendid thing it is to be your queen. Good-bye, my dear," he said gravely to Marta. "You may think me cruel now, but you will be happier among my forest friends than you can ever hope to be with wicked Malkin!"

Half terrified, half fascinated, the doll allowed herself to be led away by the excited goblins and trolls,

who hurried her through the trees until the forest swallowed up even the faintest echo of their passing.

The fury and despair of Malkin the toymaker are more easily imagined than described when he came home to find his workshop empty and his precious toy gone!

It was easy to see the way she had gone, for the window stood wide open, but nobody had seen Anders climb inside or help her out. Many a neighbor

wished he had kept his eyes open that morning, or that Malkin had had a little more confidence in his fellowmen and had asked this one or that to keep an eye on the place while he was gone.

The village of Pils was in uproar. The people had come to take pride in the work of their once unpopular craftsman. After all, he was their master toymaker and the whole village would share in his honor if he won the King's prize. One and all came to offer their condolences to the half-demented Malkin, but he repulsed them so rudely and his language was so unpleasant that they soon went away and left him alone.

Shortly after dark he sat exhausted with despair at his workbench, with his head in his hands, too miserable to eat or make himself a cup of coffee to drink.

Suddenly the sound of a feeble scratching came to his ears, followed by a sobbing on the far side of the door. Hardly able to believe his ears, Malkin ran to open it. Marta staggered across the threshold, soaked to the skin, her black hair lank and draggled, her cloak in ribbons, her new dress clinging to her limbs and wringing wet with the snow through which she had stumbled.

"Oh, Master, Master," she sobbed, sinking to the floor beside his feet.

Malkin saw that she was nearly run down. He whipped out his key on its silver chain.

Marta revived as the key turned in her heart.

Climbing onto her usual chair, she spread her embroidered skirts to dry in front of the fire and began to tell her story.

"...So when Anders had left me with the trolls and goblins, they dragged me away by force," she finished piteously. "And just imagine it—they wanted me to live with them underground! They certainly admired me!" She sighed. "And they showered me with wonderful presents..."

"Why didn't you bring the presents back with you?" Malkin said sharply.

"I had quite enough to do to bring myself in all that snow and rough traveling," said the doll, shedding tears of self-pity. "I really don't know how I got home at all."

"How did you escape?" Malkin demanded.

"Why, Master, in a very strange way," said Marta with a spiteful gleam in her eye. "It came up in conversation that you had made me! And this had a paralyzing effect on all those little mountain people. At once they said they did not want me to be their queen after all! They seemed to be quite angry with Anders for suggesting it. At first they said they would give me to the mountain crows who were also in need of a queen and not so particular as they were. But when I said I would go straight back to where I came from, nobody made the slightest objection or tried to stop me, so I got up and left them. The journey was terrible and it is a wonder that I got here alive! I can't think how Anders could have treated me so badly, and I never got my necklace after all."

"His brother Rudi put him up to it," Malkin brooded. "He saw my work was better than his and hoped to spoil my chances of winning the King's prize! Aha, Master Rudi! And your little brother Anders! You are not so clever as you thought yourselves to be! I'll have my revenge, you shall see! And meanwhile, my dear," he said, turning to the doll, "we must wash and press your dress, and I think until the day of the contest it would be wise for you to wear your old cotton one and your clogs, while I pack the other things in my traveling bag."

⪻ 8 ⪼

Anders and Little Janni

At his own home, Anders was so pleased with the apparent success of his adventure that even his family was surprised by his exceedingly high spirits. He soon had all the household as cheerful as himself and had nearly succeeded in coaxing a promise from Rudi that he could go with him and old Peter to the King's contest.

"But it is an eight-hour walk through the forest," Rudi protested at first.

"I can walk nine! I can walk forever," promised Anders.

"It will be bitterly cold," Rudi said, "and in places the snow is very deep."

"I have my new jacket," said Anders, "and Hans will lend me his skis which are better than mine!"

"You will be so tired," said Rudi. "Remember, when the contest is over we shall have to come all the way home again."

71

"Ah! But we will be carrying the prize with us," cried Anders, with a shout of laughter.

All the family joined in, except studious Hans, who was trying to prepare the next day's lessons at the far end of the table.

"What about Malkin's doll?" he murmured, more to sober Anders and get a little peace than for any other reason.

It did sober Anders. His secret was too important to betray, so he turned to Rudi and implored him once again to let him go to the King's palace on the day of the competition.

Rudi asked Elsa for her opinion.

"I think Anders should go," she said gently. "Hans will stay and look after me, won't you, Hans?"

"Indeed I will!" said Hans readily.

Anders rushed to kiss his sister, and Rudi announced that Margaret had offered to come and stay with her while the others were away. None of them knew quite how much unselfishness it cost Elsa to send two of her beloved brothers on such a far journey through the forest in wintertime.

Anders' spirits remained at their highest pitch. He smothered the growing feeling of guilt toward Malkin with an excess of gaiety that led him into a foolish act he would never have dreamed of in days gone by.

One day he ran across the footbridge by the millstream to visit little Janni at the mill. The millstream was all but frozen over now. It flowed with a sullen, cruel look. Anders crossed the bridge with a couple of bounds, then knocked on the door.

Janni herself opened it. He mother was out and she was all alone in the kitchen, though from above could be heard the *thud-thud* of her father, who was at work in the mill. Anders entered with a swagger. He had become so important in his own opinion that he felt rather condescending in coming to talk to a little girl like Janni.

The two children sat side by side by the stove, sharing an apple that Janni had been nibbling. It had lasted her all the morning, but it tasted much better now that Anders was taking great bites out of the other side of it. Janni had to double her bites to get her fair share.

"So in a week from now you will see me no more, Janni," Anders said grandly. "I shall be marching through the forest beside Rudi and Uncle Peter, on my way to the King's palace!"

"Is it really so soon?" said Janni, her eyes opening wide. "And are the toys quite finished?"

"Quite finished," Anders said. "Rudi put the last touches to you this morning."

"To *me?*" said little Janni.

"Yes, to *you*. He has carved you as real as life, with all the other figures dancing on top of his singing box."

"*Oh!*" cried Janni, enraptured. "If only I could see it! Have I got my Sunday pinafore on?"

"Yes," said Anders. "Elsa made all the dresses. It is just exactly like you for the Princess to see."

"Your brother is so clever." Janni sighed. "Oh, if I could only see it just once, before he takes it away!"

Janni was the only child in the village who had not seen the wonderful toys. Her parents were too busy to take her out, and she was not allowed to leave the mill by herself.

"Come back with me and I'll show you," Anders tempted her, but Janni was not so easy to persuade as Marta.

"I may never go farther than the bridge," she said gravely, shaking her head.

"Well, you had better do as your parents say," Anders agreed. Soon after, he left her. The apple was finished and he threw the core into the millstream.

When Anders came into his own house he found the kitchen empty. Rudi was out, and Elsa was in her brothers' room, getting out the warm socks and mufflers they must wear on their journey. Hans had gone to the schoolmaster's library to borrow some books. And on the table stood the finished singing box, perfectly finished and polished, all the little figures waiting, it seemed to Anders, for the moment when they could dance to a tune.

He knew better than to turn the key, but circled around and around the singing box, admiring it from every angle. Now that he felt sure Marta was out of the way, he was certain Rudi would win the King's prize. Dear Uncle Peter's house was very wonderful, but once you had seen it all, you had seen it, and that was that. Rudi's box, Anders believed, never came to an end of its marvelous selection of tunes.

It seemed a shame that little Janni could not see it now, while it was all new and shining. She would so much enjoy looking at it and admiring all the figures, even if she could not hear it play. Of course she was right to obey her parents and to stay on the other side of the stream, but what a pity she could not look at the little carved dancing Janni that Rudi had made!

Of course, thought Anders, I might carry it across the millstream and show it to her.

A few days ago such an idea would not have entered his head, but now he considered himself almost a man. How otherwise could he have outwitted Malkin without being found out, and extorted a promise from Rudi to take him all the way through the forest in wintertime to the contest at the King's palace? He felt as clever and wise as the oldest man in Drüssl.

All the same, he was glad no one was there to question him as he went out of the back door, carefully wrapping the musical box inside his jacket. He hurried down the hill but went no farther than the bridge. He did not want to be away from home for long.

"Come and see, Janni!" Anders called up to the mill. "I have something to show you!"

Janni's face looked around the millhouse door.

"What is it?" she asked.

"Look!" Anders held aloft the singing box.

The next moment Janni came flying down the slope to the bridge.

"Oh, do show me, Anders! Show me quick!"

Janni circled around the box, fascinated by all she saw.

"It is perfectly wonderful!" she breathed in awe. "And does it really play a hundred different tunes, Anders?"

"It certainly does!" said Anders proudly. "But I can't play it for you. One day your mother shall bring you to our house and Rudi will wind it up for you himself. Then you shall hear all the tunes and see the figures dance. But that will be after Rudi has won the prize, of course!"

Janni was examining the little figures.

"Look at the goblins," she said, delighted. "And the schoolmaster, and the burgomaster—and look at ME! Oh, let me hold it, Anders, just one minute by myself!"

"I don't think I ought to let you do that!" said Anders, to torment her, but the next moment he put it into her hands.

Of course, once she held it, Janni did not want to let it go, and she went on looking, first at this little figure and then at that, until Anders said he must be going home.

"Why, I've only looked at it for a minute and already you are taking it away from me," Janni complained angrily. "Don't snatch it away so soon!"

"I am *not* snatching it away from you," said Anders indignantly, "but you have held it quite long enough and it is time you gave it back to me. I *shall* snatch it from you if you won't do as I say!"

Janni was upset by the roughness of his voice and held it out of his reach.

"I shall give it back when I please," she said to him.

This made Anders furious. He leaped at her, seizing one yellow pigtail with one hand while with the other he snatched at her wrist.

Janni cried out, jerking away from him. The singing box flew out of her hands just as Anders made a jump for it.

He jumped too late, for the box vanished over the rails into the icy millstream below. Janni screamed, but her cries were drowned in a splash as Anders jumped into the water after the box.

"Oh, Father! Father!" cried Janni, running toward the mill.

Her father heard her cries and came racing down to the stream. Anders had come to the surface again, blue in the face and gasping for breath, but with something tightly clasped in his arms.

The burly miller ran down the bank to a spot where a willow overhung the water. Clinging to this with one hand, he soon fished out Anders and his prize, who had nearly perished in the icy water.

Rudi, returning home, had also heard little Janni screaming down by the bridge. He ran to the stream just as the miller appeared, carrying the dripping Anders in his arms.

Thanking his brave neighbor, Rudi took his burden from the miller and ran home to wrap Anders in blankets in front of the fire, where Elsa rubbed his limbs and Hans was sent flying to fetch something warm to drink.

Anders was unconscious, and his brother gently removed the ruined musical box from his clutching fingers. Without saying a word he put it away in a cupboard out of sight.

It was the first thing that Anders asked for when he opened his eyes and looked about him.

"Where is the box?" he cried out. "Is it still in the water?"

"The box is quite safe and unharmed," Rudi soothed him. "You saved it from the stream and I have put it away for the meantime until you are better."

"Oh, I am so very, very sorry," Anders cried, bursting into tears. "I don't know how I could do such a stupid thing! It was all my fault and nobody's else's, so you won't scold little Janni, will you, Rudi?"

"No, I will not scold Janni," Rudi promised, and presently Anders was persuaded to lie down and go to sleep. But in the morning he awoke with a fever and a heavy cold, and surprised his family by the meekness with which he accepted the fact that he would not now be able to go to the King's palace for the competition.

"I know I deserve it. It is my punishment," he said. His contrition was so pathetic that the neighbors, who had come to commiserate with Rudi over his spoiled toy, gave all their sympathy instead to Anders. They showered him with apples and sweetmeats and told each other what a brave boy he was to jump into the millstream in winter to save his brother's musical box.

The box still worked, but the gay costumes had

been spoiled by the water, and some of the paint had run. Rudi set it on the table beside Anders, repairing the faces with his brushes while Elsa fetched her box of silks and satins, sewing feverishly to make new dresses and suits.

Anders was in despair that it might not be fixed in time. "Will they be finished before the contest?" he kept asking, for his guilt nearly drove him crazy.

Janni had confessed her share in the disaster, and her mother brought her over to beg Rudi's pardon. Her parents had scolded her all evening long.

"Now say what you have to say," her mother told her sharply when she stood in front of them all, her hands twisting in and out of her apron. But Janni could not remember a word of what her father and mother had taught her. She stared and stared at the figures Rudi was patiently repairing.

"Oh, please, dear Rudi Toymaker, will you make me a clean Sunday pinafore?" she burst out at last, looking in disgust at the sodden rag the millstream had left around the wooden Janni's waist.

"At least Malkin is robbed of his revenge," said Hans gloomily when the miller and his wife had taken Janni away.

"What revenge?" asked Rudi, giving the burgomaster's cheeks a fresh brushful of paint.

"Why, everybody is saying that our Anders led Malkin's prize doll into the woods and tried to lose her," said Hans. "And Malkin says it was all your doing, Rudi, to rob him of the King's prize, although nobody believes you had anything to do with it. But Malkin has vowed to be revenged on you just the same!"

"Is this true, Anders?" asked Rudi severely, turning toward the bed, but Anders, with a faint flush of fever on his cheeks, had conveniently fallen asleep.

⋘ 9 ⋙

Malkin's Revenge

The whole village was talking about the trick Anders had played on Malkin.

They forgave him easily, because the trick had failed and because the toymaker from Pils was so unpopular. Besides, Anders' accident and illness had made him everybody's spoiled darling. While shaking their heads over his goings-on, they hunted at the same time for an apple or a little cake that they might take to him.

Only Rudi and Elsa looked at him gravely, and this distressed Anders very much. He knew he had done wrong in taking the musical box to show Janni, but as for Malkin's doll, he had stolen her for Rudi's sake, and now she was back again, so what was there to make a fuss about?

"But what is Malkin going to think of us?" Elsa reproved him gently.

Anders refused to worry himself over anything that Malkin might think. He might have been rather more concerned if he had known how the toymaker was plotting to take his revenge.

Malkin's anger was so intense that day in, day out he could think of nothing but vengeance. Even if Anders was the real culprit, Rudi was his older brother and it was on Rudi that Malkin meant to be revenged. And although Marta had been saved for the King's contest, Rudi and his entry should never get there, Malkin had promised himself. He gloated when he heard of the accident to the musical box, but soon the word went out that it was as good as new again, and Malkin went back to grinding his teeth, biting his nails, and plotting . . . plotting. . . .

The journey to the King's palace lay through deep forests where lurked an occasional wolf; but

there were very few, these days. The wolf packs of long ago had been hunted down and scattered. Those who were left hunted singly or in pairs. There was no great danger for a man traveling alone, and none at all for two.

Malkin had no fear of the long, lonely walk, although, if he had been on better terms with them, he would probably have kept company with old Peter and Rudi Toymaker. As things had turned out, he meant to take quite a different road and avoid them altogether.

Although it was winter, there really was no danger from wolves at all, but Malkin was hatching a wicked plot that would rouse the spirit of the old wolf packs, and it was not him they would be hunting in the forest.

During the last four days before the contest, nothing at all was seen of Malkin, but Marta sat and simpered in the toyshop window as if nothing had happened to her at all.

Hidden in the back of his shop, Malkin was busy with bottles, powders, and pills—grinding, brewing, and boiling over a little fire that never went out. Strange smells wafted up the chimney, strange sparks crackled in the fire, while the liquid in the pot seemed to bubble and hum in a kind of frenzy as Malkin stirred it with an iron spoon.

At the end of the fourth day, he dipped the spoon deep into the liquid and began to hunt about at the bottom of the pot. Presently he found what he wanted, and drew to the surface a small dark object no larger than a pea. As the liquid slowly ceased to bubble, Malkin picked up the small object between his finger and thumb and laid it in the palm of his left hand.

He smiled as he looked at it. From the pill arose a strange perfume, hardly noticeable to human senses but strong and challenging to the keen nose of a wolf. No wolf who caught that magic tang would stay for a moment in his lair. Once the cunning scent of that enchanted potion roused his senses he would leap up and follow—follow until he hunted it down!

This was the revenge that Malkin had planned for Rudi, and on which he had worked for four whole days. With a sly smile he put the pill in his pocket and set out in the fading light to go to Rudi's house.

Here, all was in preparation for the great journey, and Anders, out of bed for the first time, was watching Elsa as she stuffed her brother's satchel with the pies, bread, and wine she had prepared for the travelers.

Rudi had gone to old Peter Toymaker's house to fetch him over to supper and to spend the night, as they had decided to start at daybreak. The following night a cousin of Rudi's sweetheart Margaret was to give them a bed for the night. Margaret, too, was coming to supper, so that between packing the satchel and cooking the meal Elsa was fully occupied and had little time to console Anders, who was looking very dejected at the thought of being left behind and missing all the excitement of the contest.

Hans had run to a neighbor's for some herbs Elsa wanted for her soup. Anders was supposed to be stirring this, but he had fallen into a wistful daydream, and the pot swung idly over the fire.

Presently there came a *tap! tap!* on the outer door. Elsa went to open it, expecting to find yet another of the neighbors bringing good wishes for the morrow, but her face turned pale as Malkin stepped across the threshold without being invited, while Anders was so startled he looked ready to dive head first into the soup pot to conceal himself.

Malkin had twisted his face into a smile that was intended to be neighborly and pleasant. He was carrying one of Marta's little shoes in his hand.

"Sweet lady, again I beg for your help," he said to Elsa. "This little shoe—the stitches are burst. And on the very eve of the competition! I see neighbor Rudi is getting ready to make an early start like myself. But unlike him, I have no one to see me off or make things easier for me. I have to bake my own bread, pack my own sack, mend my own jacket, and turn the key on my poor little home with no one to care whether I ever come back again!"

"Give me the shoe, sir, I will mend it!" said Elsa.

Greatly embarrassed because she disliked the toy-maker so, she vanished with the slipper into an inner room.

Malkin seated himself in Rudi's chair and looked at Anders.

"Well," he began, "you haven't been near us lately, Master Anders! That was a shabby trick you played on me . . . eh?"

Anders hung his head, refusing to meet the toy-maker's gaze. He wished Elsa would finish the slipper quickly, so that Malkin would go away.

"However, I hear you are a brave boy after all," jeered Malkin, delighted to see him so discomfited. "They say you jumped into the millstream to fish out your brother's toy! You wouldn't do so much for mine, would you?"

"If Marta fell into the stream I would certainly fish her out," Anders said with spirit. "Marta is a friend of mine!"

"She doesn't think much of your friendship since you dragged her up the mountain and sold her to the trolls," said Malkin.

"I thought she would like to be a queen, and they would treat her better than you do," said Anders. "And I wanted Rudi to win the competition," he added honestly.

"Ah! You knew he would not have much chance against Malkin and his doll," said the toymaker, chuckling with pleasure. "Poor Rudi! Such a pretty box as he has made! But what child would look twice at it beside a walking, talking, singing doll?"

"If the King or the Princess knew what Marta is really like, she would never win the prize," Anders said. "She isn't very good, even now. She disobeyed you quickly enough, and I'm sure it wouldn't take much to set her off at her old games again!"

"Nonsense!" said Malkin, looking slightly alarmed. "Her works are all in perfect order now. She will win the King's prize for Malkin, and Rudi and poor old Peter Toymaker will walk all that way in vain. I hope your brother has a good warm coat. The weather is likely to be very cold. Ah, yes! I see he has a warm jacket, all patched and mended, not like poor Malkin, who must live in holes. What is this I see? A forester's badge on the pocket?"

"Take your hands off my brother's coat," Anders shouted, jumping up in anger. "You aren't fit to touch it, Malkin Toymaker! That jacket used to belong to my father, who was one of the King's foresters. Our Rudi wears it now, and presently it will come down to me. Leave it alone, I tell you!"

"Very well, sprite, I will not touch it," Malkin said, folding the coat and putting it on the back of a chair, but not before he had secretly slipped his little black pill into one of the pockets.

"Well, wish your brother good luck, my little man, for we are not likely to meet on the road. I intend to take the higher path and to start later in the day. I have no friends in the city and I cannot afford the cost of an inn!" He sighed. "So I shall be forced to walk all night!"

Anders had no sympathy to waste on Malkin. He was relieved that the toymaker did not ask to see the musical box and Uncle Peter's dolls' house, both carefully packed for the journey in a second bag. Just then Elsa came back with the mended shoe and Malkin took his leave.

Soon after, Rudi returned with Margaret and old Peter Toymaker.

Rudi's keen nose, trained in the woods, caught an unusual scent in the air.

"What are you burning in the fire?" he asked Elsa.

"Nothing except the pine logs you cut for me this morning," Elsa said. "Unless Anders has let the soup boil over."

"Indeed I have not!" said Anders indignantly, suddenly remembering his duties and beginning to stir very fast.

"Malkin came here with a slipper he wanted me to mend for his doll," said Elsa with a slight shudder of distaste.

"Ah!" said Rudi. "I thought the house smelled as if a wolf had been in it."

Anders and his brother Hans, who had just returned, were so amused at the idea of Malkin smelling like a wolf that they burst out laughing, and the evening took a cheerful turn.

Rudi and Margaret went out together to look at the stars.

"If I win the prize," Rudi said to her once more, "we shall have our own little home, sweetheart, and the next feast will be on our wedding day."

"Oh, Rudi," Margaret cried, throwing her arms around his neck. "Do take care of yourself in the forest and come safely home to me! Oh Rudi, Rudi! What's that?"

Far away in the forest came the long-drawn howl of a wolf.

Rudi looked surprised, for it had been a long time since he had heard a wolf in those parts.

"Only a lonely wolf, dearest!" he told her calmly, as he drew her back into the house and the firelight once again.

❧ *10* ❧

The Journey Begins

Rudi and old Peter left Drüssl later than they had intended, for a blizzard blew up in the night and it seemed foolish to travel until it had cleared.

Lying awake in the dark, Rudi had heard a wolf howl again, to be answered by another farther away. He was puzzled, knowing the woods so well since his early boyhood. To his knowledge there had not been any wolves in the district for years. He hoped Margaret had not heard them. She said nothing about it when they took their leave but only begged him to take his gun.

"Certainly I will," Rudi agreed, to please her. "And if I shoot a deer, you shall have a new pair of slippers made from the hide!"

He always kept a good supply of shot, but when he went to take down his powder horn from behind the door, it was not there. Angrily Rudi questioned his brothers, but neither Hans, who was already a steady shot, nor Anders, who was hardly big enough to lift the gun, knew anything about it.

The two girls searched the house in vain while Hans flew to ask the burgomaster if he had any powder to spare, and old Peter Toymaker fumed at the delay in starting.

The burgomaster willingly sent Rudi all the powder he had, which was a mere pinch in a silver flask. He had been going to ask Rudi to buy some for him in the city, he explained regretfully. Rudi was the huntsman of the village. Hardly anyone else had a gun.

Impatient to start, he did not ask any further but set out through the snow, with the good wishes of all the village ringing in his ears.

Old Peter carried the sack of food and a stick to help himself along. It had been many years since he had attempted such a walk, but his spirits were high. Rudi carried both toys in a bag around his neck and his gun over his shoulder. He would not have troubled about the lack of gunpowder if he had been alone, or if the strange sweet wolf scent had not haunted his nostrils with a fleeting sense of danger.

He set a slower pace to match the steps of the older toymaker. They traveled on steadily through the sparkling woods in the clear cold sunshine that had followed the storm.

They had a pleasant surprise at the crossroads some miles from home. Rudi's young brother Maurice, the blacksmith's apprentice, was waiting there to wish them Godspeed on their journey, and to give them a bottle of wine sent by his master.

The toymakers halted for a moment to open the wine, and to show Maurice the two wonderful toys they had with them. In exchanging news and family gossip an hour slipped by, and when they got up to go, Rudi's brother offered to walk with them for a while, his master having given him a holiday.

Rudi asked him whether any wolves had been heard of lately. Young Maurice shook his head.

"My master wanted me to bring his gun for your journey," he said. "He has just forged a new barrel for it and it is a very fine weapon. But I told him you would never use any gun but my father's, and I see you have it with you now."

"I have," said Rudi. "Only I have lost my powder horn, and all I have with me is a little that the burgomaster had to spare."

"My master offered me his flask as well," said the boy, vexed, "but I thought you always had plenty of powder."

"Well, there is very little to shoot these days," Rudi said. "The wolves are all gone, the foxes hardly worth troubling about, and one seldom sees a deer."

"The brown bear still sleeps in the cave by the white rock," said young Maurice, "but you won't be seeing *him!* Well, I must leave you now, though I would very much like to go all the way. A good journey to you both, and a safe return! I think your house will win the prize, Uncle Peter, but if it doesn't, then it will be Rudi's musical box! Good-bye, then, and good luck!"

Off he set for home at a jog trot. The blacksmith's wife would have a good dinner waiting for him and he did not want to let his dumplings get cold.

It was now midday, and a long time since the two travelers had breakfasted. They stopped to eat one of Elsa's meat pies that she had baked for them.

"We have a long way still to go!" old Peter said. "I keep you back, Rudi. You would have done better to go alone!"

"What is the haste?" Rudi asked. "We have all day to travel in and all night, too, for that matter! What does it matter if we made a late start? We shall travel steadily and eat the miles away!"

But old Peter Toymaker found the new snow heavy going. At least once every hour he needed a rest. By three o'clock only half of their journey was done, and the sun was already setting behind the mountains.

As it plunged below the pine trees, a chill like a steel blade fell on the forest. The cold met them like a weapon.

At the same time Rudi heard the first wolf's howl.

He had been listening for wolves all day. The sound did not surprise him so much here as it had done outside the village.

The cry, far far away behind them, was not answered, and old Peter did not notice it. He plodded along, a little weary now, but unwilling to ask Rudi to stop for him.

However, a little farther along, Rudi stopped of his own accord and loaded his gun.

"Why do you do that?" old Peter Toymaker asked in surprise.

"I always load my gun before it gets too dark to see," Rudi answered wisely. They went on again, and for a long, long time the forest was silent.

"I think Margaret's cousin's family will be waiting up for us!" old Peter said, the next time they stopped to rest. "They expected us by dark, I think, and we still have a great way to go. We seem to travel slower instead of faster. I wish I had let you go without me. You would have been there by now!"

"How crowded the city will be tonight!" Rudi said, to distract him. "Just think of all the people who will be there—and all the toys. All the carts and horses and puppets and clowns and theaters and tops and hoops and balls. What a dream city for children! How much our Anders and little Janni would enjoy it all!"

Old Peter began to plan what he would take back to the children left behind—sweetmeats, dolls, drums, cakes, and candies. In fact, so many good things were planned for them by their good friend that he would have needed at least two more sacks to carry them in.

But while he was thinking and planning, a sound came to his ears that Rudi had been aware of for quite a little while past.

"Why, Rudi," old Peter said in surprise. "Surely that is a wolf I hear howling in the distance?"

"Yes, I think it is," Rudi said, in a matter-of-fact tone, but his fingers tightened on the gun under his arm. "Are you warm enough, Uncle Peter? Are you tired? Are you cold?"

"I am warm enough," Peter Toymaker replied, "and I am not so very tired. The last time I heard the wolves howl, Rudi, was the winter when you came to me. You were such a little fellow, and I used to worry about you walking through the forest alone!"

"I wasn't afraid," said Rudi. "And I had no gun in those days, either! Do you remember you told me to learn the ways of all the animals and birds in the forest, till I was cleverer than they were? And to make friends with the trolls and the goblins? Many and many a time that advice has helped me! But they don't have much to say to me now that I am a grown man. It's Anders they run after these days."

"Anders has not your forest sense," old Peter said. Rudi's keen ears could hear not one wolf, but several, some near, some distant, and at least one coming closer and closer.

"Anders is younger than I was then," he said, keeping up the conversation to keep the sound from old Peter's ears while at the same time he urged him ever so gently forward. "And he has always had time to play. When he settles down to work, he will do as well as the others. He has a good heart, with all his faults."

The wolves howled again. Old Peter looked anxiously behind him.

"Don't worry, Uncle Peter," Rudi said. "The wolves don't hunt in packs these days. There will be a full moon tonight and the few remaining wolves are feeling restless. They won't trouble us, I can assure you."

But all the same he kept a good lookout ahead of them and to the rear. He wished the burgomaster had not been so careless about his gunpowder supply.

Far away, on a higher track behind them, a long way off, Malkin too heard the cry of the wolves. He was traveling with his doll, who shivered a little in her thin cloak and cotton dress and clogs. Her slippers and her pretty clothes were packed in a bag carried by her master.

Malkin listened and smiled to himself as more and more wolves joined in the hunting cry that was rising to a chorus.

Old Peter quickened his pace, until he became so breathless that he had to pause.

"Don't press yourself so," Rudi advised him. "We shall do no better if we proceed by fits and starts. You may rest assured that if a wolf appears I shall shoot him through the head. But do not wait for me if I stop and fire—make your way forward. I do not think the creatures will dream of attacking us. I haven't heard of them attacking travelers for many a year, and there are two of us, remember! I hope they will not molest neighbor Malkin, either, who is traveling alone."

"As *you* should be!" moaned old Peter Toymaker. "I am a selfish old man, as I now see clearly, and you would be much safer without me dragging at your heels and hindering you. The King's prize, too—that is a contest for young men, not old graybeards like me. What good can it do me if I win? And now it seems I have risked both our lives through my vanity and thoughtlessness!"

Rudi gently took his arm so that the old man's weight rested on it.

"Dear Uncle Peter," he said. "You do yourself an injustice and me too! Haven't we been partners through so many happy years? Isn't it our place to travel side by side to take part in the King's contest? When has anything separated us before?"

"Quite so, quite so," said old Peter. "But I need not have come with you. You could have carried both toys on your back and outstripped every wolf in the forest if I were not here to be a burden to you."

"If you talk of burdens, what did you bear for us all those years ago?" Rudi asked tenderly. "Have you forgotten how you looked after me and my sister and all my little brothers when we were young and helpless? Now I am grown tall and strong it is my privilege to serve you instead."

"Look! Look!" cried the old man in terror, suddenly glancing behind him.

Rudi leaped around. For a moment he had relaxed his guard, and now he saw the gaunt shadow of a huge wolf silently racing behind them through the trees. Nose to the ground, he leaped from pool to pool of moonlight, following their trail without a sound, as if possessed by witchcraft.

"Go on, Uncle Peter, as fast as you can," Rudi urged the old toymaker, as he slipped behind a tree, raising his gun to his shoulder.

As the wolf leaped into the next patch of moonlight, he fired, and the great beast fell dead in the snow.

A chorus of howls farther back in the forest greeted the shot, as if the hurrying pack had sensed the death of their companion and were baying for vengeance.

Rudi only stopped long enough to reload his rifle. He saw with some anxiety that he only had enough powder for two more shots.

Hurrying after old Peter, he found him so distressed with fear and overexertion that he could hardly drag himself along and gasped painfully at every breath he drew.

"Get on my back, Uncle Peter!" Rudi commanded, so firmly that the old man at once obeyed,

and in spite of his burden Rudi was able to travel faster than before. He began to weave his way in and out of the trees, making half-circles and sometimes even retracing his steps for a while before finding the track again.

After a little while the baying of the wolves ceased and completely died away.

"They are running around and around among the trees, trying to find us," Rudi said. "That was a trick I used to practice in the forest."

Old Peter was encouraged by Rudi's cleverness, and for quite a time he did not turn around to look behind them. When he did look again he cried out in terror:

"Rudi! Rudi! The wolves are almost upon us!"

Quickly putting the old man down, Rudi turned to raise his gun. Five or six wolves, running silently, were coming up the track behind them.

Bang! Rudi's shot rolled the leader over. The next stopped, howling with dismay. They hesitated, searched around uncertainly with their noses to the ground, and then loped on, but Rudi had had time to reload and pick his last shot, a great gray wolf whose pelt gleamed like silver in the moonlight.

Rudi aimed carefully and deliberately.

Bang! And the wolf fell dead.

Whether or not he was their leader, this seemed to terrify the rest of the pack. One and all turned tail and fled down the way they had come, howling fearfully, to be joined deeper in the woods by a chorus of other wolves, whose howls and yells filled the whole of the sleeping forest.

But although there was little doubt that they were still following the travelers, they dared come no closer, so Rudi proceeded as before, with old Peter riding on his shoulders, with the best speed he could make upon this dangerous journey.

"I am thankful Anders is not with us tonight," old Peter Toymaker said. "At least he is safe and sound at home!"

Rudi too was thankful that his younger brother had escaped the dangers of such a journey. How he could have looked after the two of them he did not know.

"Hadn't you better load your gun again, Rudi?"

"I won't stop unless they come closer," Rudi answered. He did not want to tell the old man that his last pinch of powder was gone. Already he had a new idea in his head.

"Is there any food left in the sack?" he asked.

"Why, yes, there is a meat pie and some bread, I think," the old man said. "Are you hungry? All my own appetite is gone, and I can't think about eating until we are safely arrived in the city."

"No, I am not hungry, but the food may be useful all the same," Rudi said. "Give it to me."

Old Peter put the food into his hands. Rudi threw it on the ground, spreading it to right and left among the trees, so that the animals would have to search for it.

Presently they heard a snapping and snarling behind them as the creatures came upon the food, growling and fighting for it in their greed.

Rudi and old Peter had put a good distance between them before the hunting chorus began again.

"Put me down and load your gun," the old toymaker begged. "I am rested and can walk again now. You will be ready to fire again when the time comes to do so."

Rudi set the old man on his feet, and went through the motions of loading his gun with a heart as heavy as lead.

"I will throw away the sack," old Peter said. "There is no more food, but the crumbs may keep them busy for a little while."

The wolves soon found the sack. With snarls of hunger they devoured the crumbs, tore the sack to pieces, and followed on their way.

"They are close behind us now," panted old Peter, though the wolves were not yet in sight on the trail behind them. "Why don't you stop and get ready to shoot, Rudi?"

"I have no more powder left," Rudi said simply. "But a mile farther on there is a large cave where we can shelter for the rest of the night. Once there, I can use my gun as a club to defend the doorway, and

we can build a fire in the entrance that will keep the wolves away. Only a little farther and we shall be safe!"

But the old man was so dumbfounded by the news of Rudi's empty flask that his legs gave way underneath him, and he would have fallen to the ground if Rudi had not caught him and hoisted him onto his back again.

"Now we are finished," moaned the old toymaker as the baying of the wolves came nearer and nearer.

But Rudi was fumbling in the sack he carried. Out of it he threw first his extra pair of gloves, then a muffler, and then the socks Elsa had so carefully darned for him. One by one he threw them down in the snow, and shortly afterward the broken chorus and the growlings, snarlings, and snappings spoke for themselves as the wolves discovered them and tore them to pieces in the snow. Every precious moment gained gave them a shred of hope, and finally Rudi threw away the bag.

"Now there is nothing left except our toys," he said ruefully.

"Our toys!" exclaimed old Peter in relief. "Then we still have a chance to save our lives! Throw them one of my fine fat painted cows, Rudi! Even the burgomaster said they looked alive! Surely they will deceive a pack of wolves!"

Rudi fumbled at the string that tied the sack of toys around his neck.

"We have barely a mile to go before the cave," he murmured, quickening his steps.

"And I have four cows," said old Peter. "Throw one every now and again and we shall be saved!"

Rudi put his hand inside the bag, but what he drew out was not one of old Peter's cows but one of the figures from the top of his own singing box. "Better my toy than his," he said to himself. Old Peter had no suspicions as Rudi flung it far into the snow.

Nearer and nearer came the wolves. Then there was a sudden silence as they examined this new object with interest. But although they licked it in turns, and rolled it over and over, they left the little figure of the baker of Drüssl lying in the snow. The wood was so hard and tasteless it was not even worth their while to pull it to pieces.

"Throw out another cow," old Peter said, as the wolves took up the chase again.

Rudi drew the miller out of his bag.

The miller had rosy cheeks and his hands were covered with flour. He looked good enough to eat, but he proved to be just as tasteless as the baker.

A little farther on, the wolves found the wooden burgomaster, but when each of them had turned him over, they left him lying on his face in the moonlight.

"How much farther to the cave?" old Peter asked Rudi.

"About half a mile," Rudi replied bravely. His shoulders were aching and his legs very weary.

"Throw out the last cow," old Peter ordered.

The soldier occupied the wolves for barely half a minute.

"What are you throwing out now?" old Peter asked as the second soldier went after it.

"Only a little hay from the stall."

"And now?"

"Some straw from the roof."

"What, is there so much hay and straw left in my poor dolls' house?" asked the old toymaker, as one by one Rudi threw his own figures away. "Hurry, Rudi! hurry! I can see them coming now! Throw it all away! There is not a moment to lose!"

But every figure was gone from the top of Rudi's musical box except little Janni in her Sunday pinafore, and even in a moment of such danger Rudi could not find the heart to throw her away. It would be like betraying Anders, he thought.

And now, ahead of them in the moonlight there gleamed the white rocks of a great cave in the forest. Only a hundred paces more and they would be safe!

"Rudi! Rudi! They are upon us!" cried old Peter, as the spatter of wolf feet behind them sounded like the coming of a gale of wind. "Oh, we are lost! Lost! Lost!"

Quickly Rudi set him on the ground.

"Run to the cave—run!" he commanded, and half dead with fear the old man tottered away toward the entrance, while Rudi, whipping around and stripping his coat from his shoulders, stood astride the path, facing the oncoming pack.

As they surged toward him, he flung the jacket at them with all his strength. Then, picking up his gun again, he raced for the cave, which he reached only a pace behind old Peter.

He turned around, holding his gun like a cudgel and preparing to defend their lives with his last breath, but, to his amazement, behind him on the path the strangest thing was taking place.

The wolves had seized upon the jacket, but no sooner had the leader touched it than he uttered an unearthly howl, such as Rudi had never heard uttered by man or beast. With his forepaws on the coat, he wrested the pocket from its place, swallowed something at a gulp, and vanished into the forest at the speed of lightning, with the whole pack at his heels.

And had Rudi known it, the magic of Malkin's little black pill was so powerful that they ran straight out of the kingdom, leaving it empty of wolves for more than a hundred years to come.

❦ *11* ❧

The End of the Journey

Rudi's first care was to revive old Peter, who had collapsed from shock and exhaustion on the floor of the cave. For a long time the old man trembled and shivered, begging Rudi to light a fire that would keep the wolves away for the rest of the night.

Rudi felt certain that the wolves would not return. He did not want to light a fire if he could avoid it, because this was the cave by the white rock where his brother Maurice had told him the brown bear slept the winter away, and the moon slanting through the entrance onto a great pile of brushwood showed where the creature's bedroom might be. If the bear was disturbed, he might well prove to be even more dangerous than the wolf pack.

But he thought old Peter's heart might not stand the further shock of this news, so he persuaded him gently that since time was short, it was hardly worth while going to the trouble to light a fire before going on to the city.

"At least let me make a warm bed with that pile of brushwood and have a short sleep," said the old toymaker, but Rudi dissuaded him, assuring him that the brushwood was very damp and dangerous for his rheumatism.

He was afraid that the old man's voice would awaken the bear, but fortunately old Peter was too weary to talk, and soon he fell asleep sitting on the floor of the cave, with his head on Rudi's shoulder.

As Rudi sat watching, and listening to old Peter's snores, another sound came slowly to his ears. This too was the sound of snoring, but deeper and more musical, as in the far corner of the cave the brown bear slept off his long journey through the seasons of the year.

Quietly Rudi removed his spoiled musical box from the bag, holding it for a long time in his hands. He would never have the heart, he thought, to mend it again. He would always be thinking of the first little figures left behind in the forest, to be torn to pieces by the wolves. He almost felt as if his real friends were gone. The musical box was a poor thing without the wooden dancers.

He passed a finger gently over little Janni's yellow hair and then placed the box in the shadows of a shelf that ran around the inside of the cave. Perhaps he would fetch it on their journey home—perhaps, after all, it would stay there in the cave forever.

A few minutes later old Peter awoke, anxious to depart.

"I cannot bear to think how anxious Margaret's cousins may be about our safety," he said.

"At least we shall soon be there now," said Rudi, fastening the bag once more about his neck. "For we are just at the end of the forest, and another hour's walking should see us in the city!"

In his anxiety to leave the cave without arousing the bear, Rudi completely forgot his father's jacket, lying in the snow where the wolves had left it.

❧ *12* ❧

Malkin in the Forest

Malkin the toymaker had intended to start late in the day and travel all night to the city, but he grew so impatient and restless that it was only a few hours after Rudi and old Peter left home that he too set out with Marta to begin the long journey through the forest.

And it was for this reason that Malkin heard the first howl of the wolves far away in the distance, and smiled in triumph to think of the fate he had prepared for his rivals.

It was as well he had started early. The doll's legs were short and her clogs were heavy. She sulked a little at being forced to travel in her old clothes, lagging behind and looking piteous when Malkin scolded her. He was too selfish to carry her and strode ahead, resting on a fallen tree until she caught up with him.

"One time I shall leave you behind altogether,"

114

he threatened, shortly after they had heard the first wolf's cry.

"Just as you like, Master! Only you will never win the King's prize without me," she replied calmly, and it was Malkin's turn to sulk, as for a short distance he took her hand to help her along.

Night fell on them, just as it had fallen on old Peter and Rudi, but the track which Malkin followed ran higher above the forest, and they could no longer hear the wolves.

The doll admired her shadow, flung by the moonlight on the snow. She nibbled daintily at a crust Malkin gave her but spoke very little. Every now and again he took out his little key and wound her up. Every ounce of energy in that wonderful complicated machinery invented by Malkin was needed for

walking through the snow. They walked for many hours and at last the path left the mountains and began to descend into the forest as steeply as it had climbed. It was a shorter road to the city, and if Rudi had been alone he would have taken it, but he knew it was too difficult and exacting for old Peter, so he had chosen the forest route instead.

Malkin, however, congratulated himself on his

choice when the path became easier, running down between the trees in a white ribbon to join the forest track some two miles nearer to the city than the brown bear's cave.

But before they arrived at this point a sound reached his ears that froze his very bones to the marrow. It was the terrible cry uttered by the leader of the wolf pack as he swallowed the magic pill from Rudi's pocket.

Marta screamed and would have run away, but Malkin seized her by the arm. "Listen!" he said, and the terror in his face gave place to a look of triumph. He felt certain that the cry had been the victory howl of the wolves as they overtook their prey.

But what was that?

Through the silent forest ran a sound like the wind scattering the leaves, only the snow lay deep and there were no leaves to scatter.

Through the trees came the rustle of a hundred feet born to travel quietly. Between the pineboles moved a host of shadows so elusive that one hardly saw them though one sensed their coming.

"Master! Master! Look!" cried Marta, clasping his legs with her frail little arms.

The wolf pack, on their bewitched course that would take them far beyond the bounds of the kingdom, had swerved aside at the road leading to the city, and were making for the route over the mountains, whence nothing would turn them back.

Up the forest path they came, straight upon Malkin and his helpless doll, who, had they but known it, had only to step one pace aside to let the pack go by, and every wolf would have passed without seeing them.

But Malkin had no time to be wise, nor did he think of anyone but himself. Shaking off the doll's frenzied grasp, he fled back the way they had come, with Marta stumbling and gasping at his heels and the wolves not a quarter of a mile behind them. He was so selfish that he would not even hold out a hand to help her or take her in his arms, though she weighed scarcely anything at all. Instead, he shouted to her to make off into the trees, hoping that if she did the wolves would chase after her and give him a chance to save his skin.

But the poor doll would not leave his side so long as she had enough breath to follow him, and as she began to lag farther and farther behind she begged him at least to stop for one moment and wind her up, as she was afraid her works were running down so that she would collapse altogether.

Malkin refused to listen to her pleading, and as they arrived at a tree with branches within his reach he gave a spring that landed him on the lowest of them, and he began to climb as fast as any cat.

Marta was too small to reach the branch, and her cries were of no avail.

"Go away," Malkin urged her as he climbed higher

and higher. "You will show the wolves where I am. Be off, I tell you!"

And as the wolf pack tore down the path, the unfortunate doll with a despairing cry fled among the trees into the deepest part of the forest.

Malkin thought the wolves had caught her, and shivered thankfully at his own close escape. But the pack had not so much as seen the escaping doll.

They had vanished down the track as if they had never existed.

All night long the wicked toymaker sat huddled at the top of his tree, cramped and frozen but too frightened to climb down for fear that the wolves might come back again.

The moon went down, the stars paled, and as daylight broke he climbed down at last, with aching limbs and chattering teeth, trying to stamp a little warmth into his blood in the frozen snow.

He did not know what to do next. His doll was lost, and there were many miles between him and his home. The night's experience had discouraged him from making the long journey back alone.

He decided to go on to the city and watch the competition. He could sell the doll's dresses to buy a night's lodging, and perhaps there would be someone going his way on the day after, who would keep him company.

With his shoulders hunched and a wretched air, he started to walk the last few miles to the city.

⤐ *13* ⤏

Anders' Adventure

From the moment that Rudi and old Peter had left the house, Anders had plagued the rest of his household and all his neighbors with so many anxious questions that it was surprising they had any patience left for him.

Would it snow again? Would it thaw? If it snowed, did it bring out the wolves? If it thawed, would the bears wake up hungry? Could one lose oneself in the forest? And if so, how long did it take to freeze to death?

"I should think our Rudi is old enough and wise enough to look after the pair of them without your tormenting yourself and all of us about them," said Hans.

Elsa secretly shared in Anders' anxiety, but did not betray it for fear of making him more nervous. As he could find nothing to do at home but quarrel with Hans, she sent him over to the mill with a message to the miller, telling him to stay and play with Janni for a while.

But even Janni could not cheer his spirits, and he did not stay long.

Just before he left she ran to the oak chest and took something from it. "Look what my father found beside the millstream late last night," she said.

"That? Why, that is our Rudi's powder horn!" exclaimed Anders. "And I can guess how it came to be lying there," he added fiercely. "Malkin had to cross the bridge on his way home! I would swear he stole the horn when he left our house, and meant to pitch it into the water! *That's* why Rudi could not find it!"

The miller was very concerned when he heard the story of Rudi's loss. He had not been present at the departure of the toymakers because he had been busy at the mill. He told Anders to take the horn home and keep it safe until Rudi's return.

Anders was now more anxious than ever. Inside the house he found the family a great deal too cheerful for his liking. They should not be laughing and joking, he felt, when their nearest and dearest were making so long and dangerous a journey in wintry weather.

He went to bed in dignified silence, putting Rudi's horn under his pillow. Hans and Margaret had suggested that Rudi had dropped the horn by the millstream himself. They meant to comfort Anders, but he scorned their suggestions and departed upstairs, barely deigning to take with him one of Elsa's pies for his supper.

He was soon asleep, and when he awoke his brother Hans lay snoring beside him and the moon lit up the humps and bumps on the counterpane and glittered on the roofs outside.

Something had awakened Anders. He sat up listening in bed, certain that he had heard a wolf howl! Yet the only sound that met his ears was the voice of a neighbor saying good-night to the schoolmaster in the street below, and the murmuring of Elsa and Margaret, who were still talking in their bedroom.

But it was not a dream. As he lay down, the eerie noise came again, from quite close by—from under his pillow!

Anders pulled it aside, carefully, not to awaken Hans. There lay Rudi's powder horn, and from within it came that curious howling, like an echo from somewhere or nowhere, far, far away.

He clapped it to his ear, and at once, as if he were listening to a distant world, Anders could hear what was going on all over the forest.

He could hear the footsteps of Rudi and Uncle Peter tramping through the forest, and the *tap! tap!* of old Uncle Peter's stick. He could hear the voices of Malkin and his doll climbing the higher path, with the occasional fall and clatter of a stone down the steep sides of the mountain.

And then clearly—terribly—Anders heard the wolves. . . .

His eyes widened with horror and dismay. He pressed the horn against his ear, but everything was silent now. Although he listened and listened, every sound had faded away.

He had no doubt that everything was happening just as he had heard it, and that Rudi and Uncle Peter were in terrible danger.

If he woke Hans, the prudent boy would want to rouse the burgomaster and organize a rescue party. Valuable hours would be lost and it might be too late, so without thinking of how little he himself could hope to do about it, Anders slipped out of bed, dressed himself in his thickest clothes, and crept downstairs to get his skis and let himself out of the house.

He had not eaten Elsa's pie, so he took it with him for the journey. His only weapon was his little knife, but quite undaunted he closed the house door and left the village, braving the danger and darkness of the great forest with only one thought in his head— to get to Uncle Peter and Rudi before danger overtook them, and to help them if he could.

Until lately, he had always had the company of his friends the trolls and the goblins when he walked in

the woods, but since he had tricked them with Mallin's doll they had been offended with him, and all his whistling could not coax them out.

Tonight he was afraid to whistle. The forest seemed immense and still. He didn't know if his friends were watching him from among the trees and snow-capped undergrowth, and he believed himself to be quite alone. He knew the others were hours ahead of him and he must hurry, but he refused to believe it was too late to help them if they were in danger, however far away they might be.

Presently he was so far from the village that he could not even hear the barking of a dog nor the lowing of a cow. There was only the immense quiet, like a gigantic cloak, enveloping him.

Anders could not pretend that he was not afraid. Every shadow looked like a prowling wolf—every pinebole might conceal a bear. The path was dark, running forward into blackness. His heart thumped like a cannon.

To his joy and comfort, a patch of open moonlight showed him the footprints of his brother and old Peter, frozen hard into the snow, but familiar and friendly like a message from home. They had not worn their skis, saying it was easier to walk in the soft snow of the forest, but Anders sped over the crust like a small bird. His shorter legs would have found the traveling hard without them.

Suddenly, at the crossroads, Anders found a third pair of footsteps joining the toymakers. Whose could they be? His heart missed a beat when he thought they might be Malkin's, but the footsteps wandered toward a fallen log, where all three seemed to have rested, judging by the flattened and scattered snow.

The three trails then went on side by side, and when Anders stopped to examine the third pair in a moonlit patch of snow he found the prints familiar. They reminded him of the footprints of Martin, one of his soldier brothers, and suddenly the mystery was solved, for when Martin joined the army he had given his boots to Maurice, the blacksmith's apprentice, and here they were, walking side by side with Rudi and old Peter Toymaker on the way to the city.

The three of them together couldn't come to

much harm, thought Anders hopefully, but his hopes were dashed when a little farther on he saw that Maurice had cut back through the woods, leaving the others, while the toymakers' footprints proceeded through the snow, alone.

Anders had brought Rudi's powder horn with him, but it told him nothing, although he put it to his ear at every other minute. It was as if its magic had been exhausted after that first sharp warning rousing him from sleep.

Hour after hour Anders plodded forward, with brief rests. His legs became numbed with cold and fatigue, his fingers were frozen and senseless. He went on as if in a dream, he was so tired, and the forest was so endless and so dark.

He cried a little, now and then, partly from self-pity and partly at the thought of Elsa's anxiety when she would find him gone in the morning. What would Janni say? And would the burgomaster pin up a proclamation offering a reward for his safe return? At such a thought, Anders' tears dried on his cheeks and froze into little icicles. He reached out to touch the nearest one with the tip of his tongue.

On and on, hour after hour, Anders felt as if he had been traveling through the forest all his life long. He had almost stopped thinking of the reason for his journey when suddenly in a patch of bright moonlight he saw something that made his heart bound with dismay and shock.

Over the footprints of the two travelers appeared

a set of smaller, more numerous tracks, covering the snow in a broad carpet of surging pawmarks—tracks that could only mark the passing of a pack of wolves!

And now Rudi and old Peter's footprints could only faintly be seen. Though Anders followed them with terrible anxiety, he dreaded the moment when there should be no more of them but only wolf prints left.

To his joy and pride he turned the next corner to find the body of Rudi's first wolf lying stiff in the snow.

"If only I could skin it and take home the pelt," Anders thought. "How proud everybody would be of our Rudi!"

But as he hurried on, more confident now, he suddenly realized that there was only one pair of footsteps now in the snow. Rudi's tracks were there, but old Peter Toymaker's had disappeared.

"How can this be?" Anders asked himself in dismay, but before he had dared to think that the worst might have happened he noticed that Rudi's steps were now spaced farther apart and sunken more deeply in the snow. At once he guessed what had happened. "Rudi is carrying Uncle Peter on his back," he said, and pressed gladly on.

Again there was no time to stop, and a little farther on he was not at all surprised to find the bodies of two more wolves, one the largest he had ever imagined, with a head as big as a horse, thought Anders, staring at it in the moonlight.

Presently Uncle Peter was on his feet again, and then he found a scuffling and trampling around the spot where a few crumbs remained from the bread the travelers had flung to the pack behind them. Then he found the sack itself, torn to shreds.

"Rudi must have finished his powder," Anders thought, trembling with fear. But he was so confident of his brother's will and courage that it was only when he suddenly found the figure of the little wooden baker of Drüssl lying abandoned that he really believed in the terrible danger threatening his dear ones.

"If Rudi is throwing away his toys, then he must be in fearful danger," Anders thought, picking up the little figure with tears in his eyes. Soon he came upon the miller, and put him in his pocket beside the baker. Then he found the burgomaster, followed by the soldiers, one by one.

Now he began eagerly to look forward to finding the next little carved figure, for while Rudi was still throwing them down it meant that the two toymakers were safe from the wolves.

He knew every little figure by heart. He had watched Rudi carve them and Elsa make their dresses. Now he began to look ahead for the next, and the next. He knew to his despair that there could not be many more.

And presently every little figure was accounted for except little Janni. He told himself hopefully that until he found her lying in the path, old Peter and Rudi must still be alive!

Suddenly ahead of him he saw Rudi's jacket lying in the road. Almost beside himself with grief, he picked it up—but nothing was rent or torn except the pocket. And just ahead of him loomed the entrance to a great cave, with the footprints of the two toymakers leading straight into the mouth of it.

But the tracks of the wolf pack stopped short where the coat had lain, and then branched off, suddenly, at an angle, in another direction.

They were safe! Rudi and Uncle Peter were safe! No doubt they were there inside the cave with its great white rocks shining silver in the moonlight. Anders staggered the last few steps into the cave, clutching his brother's jacket and almost sobbing in his relief at the end of the adventure.

⤜§ *14* §⤛

Anders in the City

To his bitter disappointment, Anders found the cave empty except for a great pile of brushwood in the corner.

But Uncle Peter and Rudi had been here, that was certain from their footprints, and after resting and letting the wolves go by, they must have traveled on to the city.

"And so shall I when I have had a rest," Anders thought, sitting down in the brushwood to eat his pie, after which he burrowed himself a bed and went fast asleep.

If the brown bear growled a little in his sleep at the disturbance, nobody heard it, and if the goblins and trolls, stealing into the cave during the night, stopped up his ears and lulled him into deeper and deeper slumbers, nobody knew about that either.

With the morning they were gone, and Anders awoke well rested, to push his arms into the comfortable depths of Rudi's coat sleeves, for it was frosty and cold outside. The warmth of the coat was consoling.

The first thing that met his eyes was Rudi's musical box on the shelf of the cave. He realized that Rudi must have abandoned it, since it was ruined for the competition, and he sat down in great delight to repair the damage with his knife and make it new again.

When each little figure was back again in its place, Anders went outside and found the sun higher in the sky than he had expected. He left his skis in the cave and set out for the city, wishing that he had not slept so long.

Firm and sure ahead of him ran the footprints of old Peter Toymaker and Rudi—there was no doubt that they were safe and sound.

When he came to a point in the track where the higher road from Drüssl met the lower, Anders heard the sound of sobbing.

Puzzled, he stopped to listen, and quite distinctly the sobs could be heard coming from among the trees.

"Hallo there!" he called, and to his great surprise Malkin's doll came staggering from behind the bole of a pine tree to meet him.

"Oh, is it really you, Anders? Is it really you?" she cried, clasping him around the knees. "Then you have really come just in time to save my life in this terrible forest!"

At first she could only sob pitifully when he asked her how she came to be there all alone and in such a plight, but little by little her story came out.

"You were quite right, Anders, when you said I would be better off among the mountain people than staying with such a cruel master," Marta said. "But before I tell you all you must swear to me, Anders, on all that you hold most dear, that you will take me with you and not desert me again!"

"I will not desert you again. I am sorry for the trick I played on you," Anders said. "I wish I had never done it, truly I do."

"Then swear it!" the doll insisted.

"All right," Anders said. "I swear on this coat that belonged to my father once and now to Rudi that I will not leave you again in the forest."

"And you will really take me with you to the city?" she said anxiously.

"I will. I swear it."

Anders could not help thinking that all chance of the doll's winning the King's prize was gone in any case. Nobody would look twice at such a tattered, disheveled object as she now presented.

"The wolves were after us . . . Marta began. "They chased my master up a tree, but he refused to help me, and I don't know how I escaped with my life! I have been wandering around all night long! I lost my clog in a thicket and the thorns tore my cloak off my back. Can you imagine a master cruel and wicked enough to treat me so?"

"So it was you that the wolves were chasing?" Anders exclaimed.

"Why, yes, of course it was! That is, they chased us after they had caught and eaten Rudi and old Peter Toymaker."

"They did *not* catch and eat them," Anders cried loudly. "I have proof that they are safe and well and have gone on their way to the city."

"I don't see how your story can be true," said the doll, "because Malkin made a magic pill and put it into Rudi's pocket. He told me the wolves would never stop following the person who carried it until they had caught him and swallowed the pill!"

"Ah!" Anders cried triumphantly, "Look here, where the pocket has been torn away! Rudi must have

flung away his jacket to keep the wolves at bay, and
they found the pill all right, but not the way Malkin
thought they would! And so he has been well punished for his wickedness," Anders added, "for I hope
the wolves have caught and eaten him as he planned
they should catch Rudi and Uncle Peter."

"No, they did not," the doll smirked. "Malkin
climbed up a tree and the wolves ran away across the
mountains. But when the sun rose and I found
the tree again, my master was gone. He must be in
the city by now, and I hope he still has my pretty
clothes with him. How surprised he will be to see me
safe and sound! I shall not be surprised if he does not
give me quite a welcome. Come, Anders, let us hurry

on! It is getting late and we have to take our places for the competition."

Anders hesitated.

"Come along, Anders! You can't go back on your word," the doll said pettishly. "You promised not to desert me, you know!"

"I promised to take you with me," Anders said slowly, "but I shall not take you to the city. I shall take you home."

"Ah! You are afraid your precious Rudi will lose the prize," the doll jeered.

"Rudi *deserves* to win," Anders said staunchly. "And so does Uncle Peter. Malkin is an assassin and should be punished. I shall certainly take you back to where you belong."

"I am Malkin's doll and you are no better than a thief," the doll shrieked in a rage. "And how is your Rudi going to win without his box of pretty tunes that you are carrying under your arm?"

Anders had forgotten the musical box. He seized Marta roughly by the hand.

"Come with me, then!" he said, and they set out in silence for the city, whose spires and citadels could soon be seen as the trees thinned out at the edge of the forest.

Never had Anders imagined a town so vast, or so full of people. Apart from all the toymakers in the kingdom, a vast crowd had collected to witness the contest, and small excited groups clustered at every corner to peer at the marvels the craftsmen were bringing to the palace. Gasps and groans of admiration and wonder ran up and down the streets like a spring breeze.

Booths and stalls had sprung up everywhere, selling hot bread and steaming chocolate to the travelers who were arriving cold and hungry. The delicious smell of yeast and sweetness tickled Anders' nose, but he had no money to spend and had to push his way through the dawdling groups with the doll clinging to his coat tails. People took her for a very small child at her brother's heels.

Anders meant to go straight to the home of Margaret's cousins, where he hoped Rudi and Uncle Peter would be, but nobody could direct him to the street. There were so many strangers in the town, and no one had ever heard of the place he mentioned. Then he thought of going to wait for them at the King's palace, but again nobody was able to help him.

"We have only just come to the city ourselves," everybody told him. "We will find out presently— there is plenty of time! The contest does not start until midday."

But Anders felt much more alone and afraid in the city than he had in the forest, and when the doll began to cry he felt like bursting into tears himself.

"Never mind, Anders!" Marta said, controlling her sobs. "I expect we shall soon find our friends, and meanwhile I have a plan. We will earn ourselves some money and buy something to eat!"

Suddenly snatching away her hand, she began to dance in the street, so gaily and lightly that everybody stopped to look at her.

"What an exquisite child," the people murmured, watching her twinkling feet, for Marta had kicked her remaining clog into the gutter. "But *is* it a child?" they asked one another, "Look at her china-white skin and painted lips! Surely it is a doll that dances!"

And they rained coins, silver and copper, on the pavement, which the doll picked up and handed to Anders. He accepted them, not knowing what else to do.

Suddenly the crowds were thrust aside by a wrathful arm as a figure in a black cloak pushed the spectators to right and left. Malkin himself forced his way into the circle surrounding her and grabbed at Marta's tattered cloak.

She stopped dancing to collapse at his feet.

"Your key, Master! I am quite run down," she whispered piteously.

Malkin said not one word, but with one vindictive glance at Anders, he vanished into the crowd with his doll tucked underneath his arm. Anders was left more alone than ever. He dropped the coins into the cap of the first beggar he met and set off in the direction people seemed to be taking, diving under elbows, twisting his way through legs, and craning in vain to see a glimpse of the route that he ought to be taking.

He felt sure it was growing late, and his progress was so slow that presently, in desperation, he left the main thoroughfare—diving down one of the quieter streets, where he limped along doggedly in what he hoped was the right direction.

Suddenly he heard a shout behind him,

"Hallo there! Hallo there, Anders!"

For a moment he thought it was Rudi's voice, but now two pairs of shining boots clattered down the paving stones, two dazzling figures in uniforms began thumping him on the back, two extremely handsome soldiers picked him up and hugged him one after the other, and he realized these were none other than his two soldier brothers, Martin and Victor.

"Well, well," exclaimed Martin, holding him high, "when I saw our father's jacket walking down the street, I knew one of the family must be inside it! But brother Rudi didn't tell us he was bringing *you* along!

"Where are Rudi and Uncle Peter?" cried Anders.

"Why, they will be at the palace by now, setting up Uncle Peter's wonderful dolls' house!" said Victor. "They were leaving the house of his sweetheart's cousin an hour ago. Uncle Peter was in a fine state when he found Rudi had lost his toy. They had a terrible time to get here by all accounts. And have you really come all the way by yourself, young Anders? I wouldn't like to be in your boots when Rudi hears about it!"

Anders struggled out of his brother's arms and produced the musical box.

"I found the pieces in the snow and put it together again," he said simply.

The two soldiers examined the musical box with great respect and delight, but Anders was growing anxious and asked his brothers if they could tell him the way to the King's palace.

"Why, my dear fellow, we *live* there!" Martin and Victor exclaimed. "We are the King's bodyguard; only at the moment we have a few minutes off before our sentry duty. Don't be afraid, we will get you there in plenty of time for the contest. But first I am sure you would enjoy a cup of hot chocolate."

Anders had a happy moment standing between his two handsome brothers with a steaming cup in his hand as he swallowed roll after roll of bread lined with sausage. Martin and Victor dug him playfully in the ribs, telling him that the honor of Drüssl was at stake if he did not manage to eat at least one more.

Finally, with his jacket bursting and his whole body glowing and comfortable, he trotted off to the palace, where Martin and Victor left him just inside the gates, giving him a friendly push as they disappeared inside a very tall and narrow sentry box, which they appeared to own between them.

Anders followed the crowd of visitors to the banquet hall, whose great tables were now covered with the rarest toys, behind which thronged toymakers of every age and description from all over the kingdom.

Anders stood awed, not knowing which way to

turn. At last he asked a little hunchback who was polishing beautiful glass marbles with a cloth:

"Please, sir, can you tell me where I can find the toymakers of Drüssl?"

The little hunchback at once stopped polishing his marbles to cry out in loud and piercing tones,

"The toymakers of Drüssl! Where are the toymakers of Drüssl?"

And from the far side of the room Rudi's voice answered, "Here!"

Anders sped across the banquet hall, hardly pausing to thank the obliging toymaker. The next moment his arms were around Rudi's knees as over and over again he repeated to his astonished brother and old Peter Toymaker how thankful he was to find them safe and sound after the night's adventures.

Rudi's amazement at seeing him knew no bounds when Anders put into his hands the undamaged musical box. "But where did you find it? How did you come?" he kept asking.

But there was no time for Anders to tell his story. Rudi had hardly put his musical box on the table with the other toys when a fanfare of trumpets sounded at the end of the hall. The great doors flew open, and the King appeared, holding the Princess by one hand and the woodcutter's daughter by the other.

ᘛ 15 ᘚ

The Competition

The royal procession passed around the hall, smiling to all the toymakers, who bowed low in return. At the far end, resting on a sofa, the Princess's mother, the Queen, watched the proceedings.

Rudi took Anders on his shoulders so he could see better what was going on. Never in his life had he imagined seeing so many beautiful toys together in one place. They were all arranged on the tables, on red velvet cushions.

The Princess and the woodcutter's daughter ran from table to table in an ecstasy of excitement, pointing to this toy and that. Anders followed them with his eyes, his breath coming short and fast.

There was a coach and horses, the coach lined with satin, the horses harnessed with gold. There was a bow as slim as a pencil, with a quiver full of arrows, each equipped with the feathers of a different bird. There was a ball dark as the night sky and studded with diamonds in the patterns of the stars, and as

141

the ball flew through the air, the stars streamed like meteorites, appearing and vanishing in space.

There was a dolls' banquet set out on dishes no larger than a crown piece. Fowls, pies, desserts and trifles, even a boar's head, delicately glazed, were there, and nothing was made of plaster—everything was carved from wood.

There were three colored balls, one red, one green, one silver, with bells inside them. They were so light to the touch that to prevent them from flying away, their craftsman had cased them in a silver net. There was a wooden dovecote with five wooden doves in it, most prettily carved. Anders felt sure that the birds would fall a-pecking when you wound them up.

The hunchback was displaying five marbles of different sizes on his velvet cushion. Each marble had a different scene inside it. In one, Anders could see a reindeer flying through the forest.

There were finely carved wooden skittles, each with a comically painted face upon it. There was a merry-go-round with wooden horses. There was a whole regiment of toy soldiers. And there were all sorts of top and whips, and hoops and balls, and arks with all the wooden animals that could be thought of.

But the dolls were not to be described! One had never imagined such a variety of them. Naturally they appealed to the Princess and her companion more than they did to Anders, and the little girls lin-

gered for a long time in that part of the banquet hall, while he followed them impatiently with his eyes.

Suddenly he saw Marta sitting among the rest. There she sat on a velvet cushion in the beautiful clothes Elsa had made for her, looking as if her night's adventure were a bad dream that had never taken place. She wore a sweet and thoughtful expression on her face.

The two little girls went into raptures over her. Anders could see Malkin, who was lurking behind in the shadows, hugging himself and rubbing his hands with glee.

When the Princess and the woodcutter's daughter had made a round of all the toys, recess was announced, and all the toymakers went into a neighboring courtyard to eat the food that the King had provided for them. In the meantime, the two girls would make their first choices.

Six sentries mounted guard over the toys in the hall. Anders was proud to see that two of the sentries were Martin and Victor.

Rudi, old Peter, and Anders were settling themselves in a corner to eat when they were joined by the unwelcome figure of Malkin.

He seemed to be very well pleased with himself.

"I hear we shared the same dangers, neighbor Rudi, on our journey here," he said. "If I could have left home earlier in the day, we would have been safer traveling together."

Anders could hardly contain himself, but seeing him opening his mouth to speak, Malkin continued in a silky tone,

"And I have you to thank, my little man, for bringing my doll safely to the city. Poor thing! When she heard the wolves she became so frightened she struggled out of my arms. Until I saw her again, I had quite made up my mind that the wolves had got her."

Anders was not to be outfaced. He stared Malkin straight in the face as he announced,

"Rudi! Uncle Peter! You must know that Malkin tried to destroy you. Marta described to me how he put a magic pill in the pocket of Rudi's jacket so the wolves would follow him and pull you both down!"

Rudi stared, while old Peter turned pale. Several toymakers on neighboring benches turned around to listen.

Malkin protested hastily, "My child, how can you pay any attention to the silly prattling of a doll? Should I be seeking you out, my dear friends, if I had such a thing upon my conscience? And who has ever heard of a charm such as Anders is talking about? It is all a fairy tale, as you can judge for yourselves."

"The pocket is torn from Rudi's coat," Anders said loudly. His brother silenced him.

"We are all here safe and sound, and this is no time for quarreling," he said firmly. "Let us discuss this matter when the contest is over!"

When they returned to the banquet hall, some of the tables had been taken away, and the unsuccessful toymakers were leaving by other entrances. They were going to display their toys in the streets of the city, which would earn them quite a fortune by the evening.

Only some twenty-four toymakers were left in the hall with their toys, and now it was their turn to bring them, one by one, before the King to show them off.

Needless to say, the toymakers from Drüssl were among the twenty-four, and so was Malkin. His Marta sat demurely upon her velvet cushion, pretending not to notice that the Princess and the woodcutter's daughter had eyes for nothing else.

The hunchback displayed his marbles before the

King, rolling them down the table to show the shower of snow that appeared from nowhere, it seemed, and painted the scenes inside them with glistening silver.

The owner of a piping bullfinch wound up his little bird, which piped and chirruped like a live thing out of the woods. The golden coach drove gravely down the table, and the skittles that had caught Anders' fancy were set up.

He nearly burst with pride when old Peter Toymaker placed his beautiful dolls' house on the table in front of the King. It seemed as if he and the Princess and the woodcutter's daughter would never stop looking at it or pointing out something new. But they did at last, and now it was Rudi's turn to present his musical box.

This roused such enthusiasm that the other toymakers grew quite impatient, waiting while tune after tune was played for the dancers, and each little carved figure was separately examined and praised.

At last the King said the box must be put aside and the rest of the toys presented. The little Princess pouted and hardly wasted a glance on the things that followed. Her eyes kept straying back to Rudi's musical box.

Anders' heart beat high with hope, but the woodcutter's daughter looked only at old Peter's dolls' house.

Then Malkin took Marta gently by the hand and

helped her to rise. Now every eye in the room was upon her, and became round with awe and wonder as she began to speak in a clear and fluting voice that could be heard in every corner of the hall.

Curtsying deeply to the King and Queen, she began, "Your Majesties! Your Royal Highness and all present! I am a humble doll. My master is a poor toymaker who lives by the work of his hands. He has taught me all I know, and if my poor tricks and graces please you, then neither master nor I will have worked in vain."

Her lovely little face was so serious that even Anders was deceived, but Rudi flushed a little and old Peter shook his head, whether in wonder or in disbelief it was difficult to say.

"Recite, my sweet fairy," Malkin ordered her.

The doll recited. "And now sing," said her master.

The doll sang like a nightingale. Several of the audience secretly wiped tears from their eyes. Long after the end of the song there was not a sound to be heard in the hall.

At last the King put out his hand and took Marta's little white one in his own.

"You pretty, pretty child!" he said. "Are you really not made of flesh and bone but only china and wood?"

"Only china and wood," sighed the doll, drooping her head.

"What beautiful clothes she wears," said the

Princess. "Just look at her slippers," said the wood-cutter's daughter.

"She is the most wonderful toy in the room," they said together. "She must have the prize!"

"I have never seen such a masterpiece in my life," the King said. "You are greatly to be congratulated, Master Toymaker of Pils. I announce you the winner of the thousand gold pieces I have offered for the best toy to be made in my kingdom!"

Anders' eyes filled with tears and his heart nearly broke as the King took a golden purse and held it out to Malkin, who led the doll forward to receive it. But as he murmured to her, "Curtsy to the King, my pretty," a gleam of triumph, excitement, and mischief crossed her face.

Instead of taking the purse from the King, she began to dance—wildly, madly, pirouetting in ever-increasing circles that took her right to the edge of the banquet hall. In vain Malkin told her to stop; she only gyrated more madly than before, flinging her arms in the air, tossing her black locks while peal after peal of wild laughter filled the air.

At first the King and Queen, the children, and many of the toymakers smiled too. But old Peter Toymaker leaned forward with an interest as deep as his face was serious.

Around and around spun the doll, flashing past her master as he made a wild grab for her dress. Anders was so excited he was jumping up and down. As the toymaker began to chase after Marta, leaping over the tables, Anders' joy knew no bounds. When Malkin tipped and fell flat within an inch of catching the doll, Anders' peals of laughter were so infectious that half the toymakers were laughing too.

Malkin clambered to his feet and resumed the chase. He was gaining on her and had all but grasped her dress when Marta made a great spring into the middle of the table, where with one foot pointed and her head flung back, she screeched at the King with her last breath,

"Nutcrackers! Numbskull! Hobbledehoy! Your mother is a witch! Yah Boo! Marta snaps her fingers at you all! Yah! Boo! Yah! Go and teach your grandmother to suck eggs!"

With a final screech of rage and a miraculous leap

she arrived on the sill of one of the high windows around the hall, where with one last shrill laugh and a wave of her hand she dropped down into the crowd below, to disappear from sight.

At the same time the bang of a door at the opposite end of the banquet hall told the petrified audience that Malkin, seeing all was lost, had escaped from the palace in the nick of time and as fast as he could go.

As some of those present would have followed him the King held up his hand.

"Such rubbish is not worth punishing!" he announced. "Let us forget this unpleasant affair as quickly as we can and pretend it has never happened. I pronounce the Toymaker of Pils banished from my kingdom forevermore. Now we must give all our attention to the business in hand."

The Princess and the woodcutter's daughter had been greatly upset by the terrible result of their choice of prizewinner. Much subdued, they whispered to the King that the musical box and the dolls' house were both so beautiful they could not possibly make up their minds which of them ought to have the prize.

"In that case," the King announced, "there is a simple way to settle the affair. We must divide the prize in half. I think you are perfectly right, my dears, and there isn't a pin to choose between the dolls' house and the musical box. We will give the prize jointly to the toymakers of Drüssl. They at least know how to make a perfect toy, which is something we cannot say about our late neighbor, the toymaker of Pils."

With joy and pride and a deep sense of thankfulness, Anders watched Rudi and old Peter Toymaker walk up side by side to receive the King's prize.

⋘ 16 ⋙

The Toymakers'
Homecoming

The other toymakers were generous with their praise and congratulations. Rudi was so modest and old Peter so dignified that they won all hearts. Anders collected an audience of his own and told the whole story of their adventure again and again. The Princess and the woodcutter's daughter were among his most attentive listeners.

When the King had shaken hands with every competitor left in the hall, he ordered that the other twenty-one should be given twenty crowns each and allowed to display the King's seal in their workshops. Then the King and Queen retired while the toymakers slowly packed up their toys and went on their way.

Martin and Victor were promptly given three days' leave by their commanding officer to celebrate the family's triumph. They decided to accompany old Peter and their brothers back to Drüssl in the morning.

The triumph of their homecoming can be well imagined. Rudi tramped the now familiar track with his father's jacket safe upon his shoulders and his powder horn well filled with powder for future hunting expeditions. Old Peter stepped out as strongly as any schoolboy and joined with Anders in pointing out the landmarks of their adventures to the soldier brothers.

The dead wolves were stiff by now. The three young men each shouldered one to carry home to the village. At the crossroads young Maurice was waiting for them. Earlier travelers had sent the news flying ahead, so that at the entrance to the village there hung a great banner, slung between two poles:

WELCOME TO
THE TOYMAKERS OF DRÜSSL!

Beneath it waited the burgomaster, with all the village at his heels—Elsa enthroned in her chair, glowing with pride, Margaret weeping for joy at seeing Rudi again, Hans, a little envious of Anders' adventures, and even little Janni by her mother's side, wondering whether her friend would be too grand to play with her now.

The homecoming began with speeches and ended in a great feast, at which Rudi's musical box played a great many tunes and old Peter's dolls' house was admired again and again.

So ended the great journey. Not long after, Rudi
and Margaret were married, to the great joy of Elsa,
the five brothers, and old Peter Toymaker, who now
had a pretty adopted niece to help care for him. And
it was not long till there were some roly-poly young
children to play in his shavings and ride on his knee.

Anders treated his nephews and nieces in a grave
and fatherly manner, and when their clamor was too
much for his growing dignity he would stroll across
to the mill to share an apple with Janni. Sitting side by
side, with their backs against the stove, he recounted
again and again the story she was never tired of hear-

ing—the thrilling adventure of the journey through the forest.

"And what happened to Malkin and his doll?" Janni always asked, no matter how often she had heard it.

"So far as I know," Anders told her, "they were never seen again."